Nazareth, North Dakota

a novel

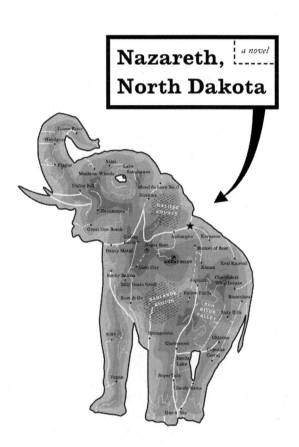

Nazareth, *a novel*
North Dakota

TOMMY ZURHELLEN

An Atticus Trade Paperback Original

Atticus Books LLC
3766 Howard Avenue, Suite 202
Kensington MD 20895
http://atticusbooksonline.com

"Song of Mary" (as "Motel de Love No. 3") first appeared in *Quarterly West*
and "Song of Simeon" first appeared in *Red Mountain Review*.

ISBN-13: 978-0-9845105-6-6
ISBN-10: 0-9845105-6-7

Typeset in Fairfield
Cover design by Jamie Keenan

ACKNOWLEDGEMENTS

Thanks to the literary journals that previously published sections of this book as individual stories, sometimes in slightly different form: "Song of Mary" in *Quarterly West* (as "Motel de Love No. 3") and "Song of Simeon" in *Red Mountain Review*.

Thanks also to the Vermont Studio Center in Johnson, Vermont, for granting me an artist's residency to complete parts of this book, and to the Starr Library in Rhinebeck, New York, and the Crosby Public Library in Crosby, North Dakota, for the gracious use of their space and resources.

Thanks to Dan Cafaro and his team at Atticus Books for believing in a quirky little book.

Thanks to all my friends and colleagues who helped me along the way, especially Baker Lawley, Lea Graham, and Jody Gehrman.

Special thanks to my family: Mom, Dad, Owen, John, and Jeff.

And finally, thanks to Charlie Cerussi, for punching me right in the nose.

for G-Ma
who danced with Cary Grant

CONTENTS

Therefore the Lord himself will give you a sign: Behold, the virgin shall conceive and bear a son, and shall call his name Immanuel.

—*Isaiah 7:14*

Brother, you say there is but one way to worship and serve the Great Spirit. If there is but one religion, why do you white people differ so much about it? Why do not all agree, as you can all read the book?

—*Chief Red Jacket, 1805*

The Annunciation

Listen: this ain't a story about a messiah. This is a story about the world coming to an end.

I ain't no storyteller; I'll leave the tale to folks who want to tell it. Only thing I want is revenge. In the old days, they used to call me Accuser or Adversary. Nowadays I'm just a dirty son of a bitch. Still get blamed for just about everything, though: plague, drought, skin disease, dead livestock, epilepsy, muggings, pornography, traffic jams, heavy metal, cocaine—fucking cholesterol—meteor showers, wife-swapping, shipwrecks, condoms, AIDS. Now it's true I done some things, but one thing I ain't is a murderer. Wasn't me who drowned the world. Wasn't me who turned the rivers of Egypt into blood. Wasn't me who destroyed Jericho and Babylon, Dresden and Nagasaki. Hell, I'm just a prisoner. Just an old soldier from a forgotten war marooned on this rock while it sinks into a cold sea.

I got my last chance for revenge.

Tonight I'm riding a lonely strip of nowhere called Highway 5, west into North Dakota. I'm drafting behind a slow convoy of big rigs that must be some kind of traveling circus; I'd pass them, but I really ain't in no hurry. They got a trailer bringing up the rear painted with all kinds of stars and planets and meteors for the fortune-tellers: *Melchior the Magnificent, Balthazar the All-Knowing, The Great Gaspar.* Wonder what old Melchior would say if he could read my hand. Up ahead I can see an elephant sticking his trunk out into the cool night air. The whole scene makes me nostalgic for the old days; there ain't many of these mud shows left, old-time traveling carnivals that pick up in the night to go from podunk town to podunk town. Old Shakespeare said *all the world's a stage*, but he ain't never seen North Dakota.

Tonight we're all following the evening star. It's a clear sky, and the sharp air hitting my face makes me feel like I can fly again. These days, riding this fatboy against the wind is about as close to a pair of wings as I can get. But not for long.

Somewhere in North Dakota, a child's about to be born. When I find him, I'm going to wait until the moment's right. I'm going to make him wish he was dead, like old Job. I'm going to whisper into his pretty ear until he betrays everybody who ever cared for him, like Eve. If I win, this old prisoner gets a midnight pardon. If I lose . . . well, I guess it's like the book says: Earth gets its Alpha and Omega, and my words here turn into a last will and testament.

Tonight I spit on your Alpha. I piss on your Omega. This story's got no beginning, and it's sure as hell not going to have an end. Stories and poems ain't nothing but recycled time anyway, just graveyards filled with the bones of past lives all lumped together in the dirt. Poetry ain't nothing but dusty monuments built on top of the dead. Pretty soon this world's going to run out of poems and stories just like trees and oil, water and air. Hell if I'm going to be the one left here alone while everybody else is shown the way to paradise. As long as I'm able to ride across this earth, you better believe there's still war up in heaven. There's still time to change the story. There's still time for one last song of retribution. There's still time for a wayfaring stranger to travel this world of woe.

Tonight I am the Angel of Retribution and I'm headed west, following the evening star into the Badlands.

Tonight I'm the Serpent hunting the prairie for the newborn Son of God.

Song of Mary

Winter 1983

I wake up when Dill rolls us into the parking lot of this neon pink fleabag off I-94, and it comes to me: in the entire history of civilization, nothing good has ever happened at a motel. Maybe it came to me last summer when I saw *Officer and a Gentleman*, when David Keith hangs himself in the motel bathroom. Or maybe I've known there was a curse all along; I was only a little girl at the time, but I know they gunned down Martin Luther King at some joint called the *Lorraine*. And this one we pull into outside Bismarck, with its doors painted the color of flamingo wings and the neon heart of a sign beating out *Motel de Love No. 3*, looks about as cursed as any place can get.

"This place is a dump," I say. "There's a Super 8 across the interstate."

"They're full up. Besides, that's owned by some mega-corporation," Dill says. "Me, I'm for supporting the little guy, the local guy."

"Local? We're about three hundred miles from anything local, Dill."

"Come on, Rox," he says, pointing up at the motel sign through the rain-streaked windshield, "it says number *three*. You think these people would be able to put up a third motel if they weren't doing something right?"

"Sure, they got a fucking monopoly."

The fact that it was the third in a chain of *Motels de Love* isn't any comfort: my brother Eggs came out of my mother third, behind me and Louise, and he turned out God awful. But I'm tired: we had six hours in the van, three weeks of fighting, and two years in a marriage that seems so hopeless at times that neither of us ever really does much to make things any better.

This weekend we got away so we could "make things work." To be honest, I'm so tired of people always saying that, we're "working it out," making it sound like love is something you can get running again if you read the manual long enough or just tinker with it, the same as fixing a toaster or patching a radiator hose. People can't even turn on the TV by themselves these days, and they think they can get a handle on love. I'm no good at it either, but at least I admit it.

When we had troubles before, Dill and me, I'd be the one to leave town for a few days, usually to circle the wagons with Louise and Annie up at the house in Nazareth. When that happens, Annie ends up cooking this giant breakfast that usually sits out cold until it gets thrown away, and while the three of us sit and drink coffee out of ladybug mugs, she always says things like, "I'm just glad I've got both my girls home, that's all." But this time Dill says he wants to pick a neutral site where we can get back to where we used to be—wherever the hell that is. He says he's got a feeling this time, a real good feeling things will all work out. "Let's just work it out," he says to me. All week he was persistent as he's ever been, and at the time I didn't know why. I go along with it because I want to believe him.

"I don't know why we have to drive three hundred miles to make peace," I say.

"Don't you ever like just starting things fresh?" Dill picks his wallet up off the dash. "Sit tight," he says, and with that, he slides off his seat and out of the van. I watch him shuffle across the parking lot towards the office. Dill always reminds me of a Fisher-Price weeble when he walks, weaving back and forth with the slow list of a comfortable rocking chair. That might be why I choose to stick with him in the first place: Dill is comfortable, an overstuffed mattress of a man, and after a good twelve or thirteen-year run of hard cases—*Gas' n' Sip* guys, we used to call them—I thought he seemed like a nice place to land. When we met, I was still waiting tables at the Flying J outside Bismarck, and he had just done some time up at James River, like most of the men in my life. But Dill really seemed to care when it came time to talk about the answers to the hard questions: the reason why North Dakota had taken back my driver's license for good. The reason why I had never really wanted to know my father. The reason I could never have kids of my own, even if I wanted to: when I was a year out of high school I had an abortion. That story has always been the hardest to tell. Dill listened.

I want to be careful not to kick a man when he's down, especially now, but there's one thing you have to know about Dill and me before the rest of this story can start making any sense. I'll put it this way: if Dill was a used car, he'd have the sign on his dash that reads *"HONEY OF A DEAL,"* the car that never seems to move off the lot even though it looks like the safe bet. But one way or the other, I always get pressured into buying a lemon.

I keep my eyes on Dill as he comes back from the office; I don't believe it at first, but it looks as if he's actually *skipping* across the parking lot. He taps on my window. "I'll grab our gear," he says, "and I've got to make a quick phone call. You go on up. It's number 207."

"Were you skipping?"

"Was I?" He smiles with his crooked teeth, and then takes in a big breath through his nose. "This place is great, Roxy. There's a pool around back, it's heated. And they even make up each room with its own love theme. You know, from the movies. Wild, right?"

I look straight ahead and sigh. "What's our theme, Dill?"

He opens the door and hands me the room key. "Surprise yourself."

"I don't want surprises," I say, ripping off my seatbelt. "I just want sleep."

"Who knows," Dill says. "Maybe you'll get both."

They let us loose in something called the *Here to Eternity* Suite. Someone had painted a panoramic beach scene on the walls, with the usual rocks and sand and fruit-stripe umbrellas, but it doesn't take me long to realize this is a nude beach, so now and then along the view you get some giddy gal being chased behind the dresser or prancing above the bathroom door with breasts bouncing around that would probably translate into the range of 34 triple Q if she were alive. There's about twenty plaster seagulls gently swinging from the ceiling on fishing line, the heating unit chugging out a constant tropic breeze, and right in the middle of the place is the bed, this Zamboni-sized waterbed propped up so high in the air that you have to use these faux stone steps just to climb into it. There's a metal box mounted on the wall behind it with a button labeled *Wave Motion*.

I hear Dill stumbling through the door, and I turn to him with my hands on my hips to give him a stare.

"I didn't have a choice," he says. "It was either this, or *Phantom of the Opera*."

"Claude Rains." I think about it for a moment, then nod. "Good move."

Dill drops the bags and looks around. "It could be worse, Rox," he says. "Couple next door has a baby, and they got stuck with *Last Tango in Paris*."

"I don't know about that," I say. "Did you get a look at the guy? He probably called ahead and requested it." I smile. "Guess what he does for a living."

"Let's see, let's see," Dill says, going through the mental picture. "Looks about thirty, ten-year-old *Grand Funk* tour shirt, scraggly sideburns, voice ruined by cigarettes." He scratches his scraggly head. "No doubt about it. He's an ex-roadie for a *KISS* cover band."

"Warm."

Dill lifts his hand above his head and raises two fingers as horns, the international heavy metal sign. "He's a drummer in a *band*," he says, and when he gets to the word "*band*" his voice comes out in an ear-splitting falsetto I always hoped I'd only hear coming from the shower.

"You're good," I say.

Dill is down wrestling our stuff out of the van when I run into the couple next door again. They have a baby with them—a boy they tell me—although it's wrapped so tight in a blanket I really can't tell. It's pink and quiet. From the shape of the woman, it looks like they got another one on the way.

The guy doesn't say anything, really, and I'm glad, because just from the looks of him I know I'm not in the mood, but the girl makes an effort to stop and talk to me. She tells me her name, Mae, and she says they're on their way up to Grand Forks for an audition with some band, or some story like that. She is young, young enough to still call me *ma'am* without really thinking about it, the way kids are told to in all the lousy jobs teenagers have to settle for these days, and with a smile. And what a smile. This Mae, this girl who at her age already has two kids and a gorilla for a husband checked off on her list, has a smile that you just know had to win every damn Sugar Beet Pageant and Sorghum Queen contest in the tricounty area. Back when her luggage rack wasn't so full.

"What's his name?" I ask, tugging at the boy's knit cap.

Mae suddenly looks nervous. "It's still up in the air," she says quickly.

"How old is he?"

"Going on six months."

That's a long time, I think, for somebody not to have a name, even in North Dakota, where sometimes you drive past an entire *town* without a name.

Her husband grunts from inside their room, and she shuffles back in from the cold and closes the door, leaving me alone to talk to myself on the soggy balcony of a motel.

I laugh a little laugh to myself, because I remember I've been there before.

I am a girl who knows her way around a motel.

I'm getting better and better at admitting things. There are some that come easy, and then there are other things that I might never get out. When I stood up at my first meeting, admitting I was a drunk was easy: my name is Roxy B., and I am an alcoholic. But the rest has been hard, trying to deal with all the things in life you can't forget, the things you know you would have done, sober or not, that shame you to the core, that put your heart in a squeeze now and then when something you see or hear reminds you of the past.

And sometimes I think getting sober makes it all worse: I find myself still wanting the same things, holding on to the same desperate men, with or without booze's warm, electric ooze that softens your heart and rounds out all the edges.

I'll admit that my first love was alcohol. I don't think I'm ready to admit it's been my only love. It makes your world smaller, something you think you can handle. It makes the lines you've heard a thousand times hit your ears like poetry. It makes all those nights you spend with lovers seem more like love.

Dill comes out of the bathroom with Bermuda shorts and flip-flops. "Surf's up, baby."

"It's January, and you want to swim. What's got into you, Dill?" I keep unpacking, trying not to look at him. "And did you just call me *baby*?"

"Get a *good* look," he says, turning in a circle. "This is the *new* me. The new me doesn't sweat the small stuff. The new me belly flops into the pool whenever he feels like it." Then he goes and flexes his muscles for me even though we both know he doesn't have any, but it's good for a laugh, since when he does that it always comes out looking like he's having a seizure.

He crosses his arms across the snowdrift of his white belly. "Laugh all you want. From this weekend on, I'm going to be the new me, the super Dill. You'll fall in love with me all over again." He comes over and slides his arms around my waist. "Let's not go back home, Rox. What do you say? We'll just keep going, the two of us. You, me, the van, and the open road." He kisses me on the neck. "But first, a dip."

"You're acting crazy. You'll freeze to death out there. Stay in here and keep the old me warm."

He waves his finger, and moves to the door. He starts to sing, "for those times they're a-changing."

There's this look in his eyes I haven't seen before. Now this is going to sound stupid, but I swear it's the same open-eyed stare the celebrities get on *Hollywood Squares* when they know the answer but they want the contestant to think they don't. Basically, bad actors doing a bad job of acting. Dill is bad at a lot of things, not just acting: singing, driving, remembering. And for all his goofy charm he's about as bad at telling the truth as I am at wanting to hear it.

It's funny how you remember things: addresses, recipes, old songs. Dill had been singing that Dylan tune the entire trip, and at the time I just thought he had it in his head, like we all do when we get a song in our heads and can't get rid of it until we concentrate on something else, like it is with the hiccups. But looking back, I figure he might have had other reasons. I guess he passed it on to me, that song, because after that weekend it took me a long time to get it out of my head. I don't remember all the words, but I know the last line says something about sinking like a stone, and that's Dill, all the way.

Mae is leaning out on the balcony, looking at the interstate traffic sail by a few hundred yards off. I offer her a cigarette. She takes the first drag like a pro.

"I shouldn't be smoking these," she says. "Bad for the baby and all."

"Live a little," I say.

Mae lifts her foot into one of the diamond-shaped slots in the railing and flicks her ash over the side. She takes another long drag. "I was looking at the map they got downstairs on the wall—you know, the big plastic one with all the roads and states and monuments and all."

"Yeah, I saw it. There's a giant cowboy hat where Wyoming should be."

Mae nods and points out towards the highway. "See the interstate? That's I-94. If you go up there and make a left and just keep going, it'll take you all the way to the ocean. And if you go up there and make a right, it still takes you all the way to the ocean. Either way, you can't lose. Isn't that amazing? I mean, that road *right there*."

"Sometimes it's hard to believe you can get to the ocean from here."

"I know," she says, taking another drag. "I wonder if people who live by the ocean feel that way about us. About here, I mean."

"I doubt it," I say. "There are plenty of places to see on that map, honey, but this isn't one of them."

"Well, if I ever got to the ocean, I'd never leave. You couldn't make me leave, ever. I'd just spend the whole day floating around. On my back. Clothes and all."

"Sounds wonderful, Mae," I say. "I hope you get there. You taking the boy and his father along, too?"

"Oh, he's not the father," she says, looking around the balcony like we're a couple of spies. "He's my husband, but he damn sure ain't the father." She goes back to staring at the traffic on the interstate.

Out of the corner of my eye, I've been keeping tabs on Dill down at the pool. He's the only one in there, of course, and I know he's been trying to get my attention for a while, standing by the pool and waving his arms like someone lost at sea, but I keep ignoring him. Finally, he cups his hands around his mouth and yells up at us.

"Baby," he says. "Baby, check this out." He has this dumb smile on his face.

"Dill, cut it out."

He rubs his hands together and takes a few steps back from the edge. "This one's for you, Rox," he says. "One triple belly buster, coming up."

"All right, Evel Knievel," I say, rolling my eyes.

Mae giggles.

"I'm watching," I say, turning around to face Mae. I take a last drag off my cigarette. "This may take a while," I say to her.

Mae lowers her voice. "Do you have kids, Roxy? You and your husband?"

Her question takes me by surprise. "No," I say. "No kids. Not that it's any of your business."

"I'm sorry," she says. She looks right into my eyes. "You'd be a great mom, though. Really." And just as she says this, before I can answer with *"Why would you say a thing like that?"* I hear the splash from the pool, and I get ready to turn back in time to give Dill his half-assed cheer, but a second or two later there comes this terrible scream, Dill's voice like I've never heard it before, like a tea kettle from hell, and when I look down at him he's standing there in waist-deep water clutching his hands to his face. He keeps screaming, and soon everybody within earshot comes out of their rooms to see what the ruckus is about. I can't tell what's wrong at first. But when I get down there and help drag him out of the water, he buries his face into my shoulder.

"My eyes," Dill says, keeping them closed. "My eyes."

Motels always remind me of my father. He was a drunk, too, a real whiskey drinker, which is why he up and joined the Gideons right after Eggs was born. The Gideons are those people who leave the good book in your motel room, kind of like backdoor JWs. Annie likes to say he found the Lord, which is supposed to make us feel better, but the more I know about all the different flavors of Lord-lovers out there, the more I know all he found was an excuse to leave. I've seen that so often at meetings, when they say you have to surrender to your "higher power," which pretty much means you surrender to the

Lord, so after a few months of meetings you either go ga-ga for God or you don't.

As far as I know he's still out there, my father, dropping off those books like some kind of born-again Johnny Appleseed. Every time I find myself in a motel, which is often, I check the drawer to see that it's there, tucked away like a sleeping child, and I wonder if my father had been the one to plant it. Most of the time I'll find one that seems brand new, like it was placed yesterday. I've promised myself to read more of it, maybe see what all I'm missing out on, but when I do I'll get stuck at the same place, about fifteen pages into the thing, where so-and-so begat so-and-so begat so-and-so, and I fall asleep.

I would tell you his name, my father, but honestly I don't think he matters that much. The closest I will ever come to the man is a one-in-five-hundred chance of touching the same book he has touched, and nobody should have to give a person credit for that.

Standing together in the emergency room lobby, the paramedic who rode in with us can tell I'm more than a little riled. He tries to smooth things. "Simple mistake, really." Turns out the night manager at the motel, this kid about eighteen, misreads the directions for chlorinating the pool; seems every night for the last couple of weeks he's been unloading a whole barrel of *HTH* in the water, which if you do the math comes to about eight months' worth of chlorine dumped into the pool at once.

The doctor kind of laughs at the whole thing. "His eyes'll be fine in a day, maybe two. Just needs a little rest is all. Avoid any light."

I want to leave for home right then and there, but with Dill's eyes out of commission, I figure we aren't going anywhere since I don't have a license anymore.

If I knew what kind of mess Dill would get us into this weekend, I'd have driven away a lot earlier than I did.

Now, I've seen so many of the old cartoons where someone leaves a baby outside the door, and the way they show it, it's really not like that at all. And it's not like they tell it in scripture, either. I've seen that old movie where Moses gets sent down the river as a baby, and they've got it all wrong. They make it look like the baby just hangs out waiting to be found by the people meant to find him, smoking a cigarette or patiently catching up on some sleep: I mean, from reading about Moses you'd think the kid was bass fishing down the damn Nile with a box lunch and a parasol. I have to tell you, that's not the way it happens at all.

I just open the door and there he is, Mae's boy, the kid with no name, left outside our room in the middle of a North Dakota winter. And boy, he isn't happy about it. He's strapped into a car seat, and his little legs and arms are flailing like a turtle turned over on his plastic shell. I half expect there to be a note, something like *"Please take care of my boy"* safety-pinned to his blanket, like you always find in the movies.

Who does this anymore? When's the last time someone creeps up to a doorstep, leaves their child, and steals away, fully hoping that the people inside take the kid in and love it for the rest of its life? Nowadays, you read about babies being left behind in a dumpster or in a bathroom stall in the middle of the junior prom, and it makes you wonder about where we're headed, all of us. Right then, I want to hate Mae, and not because I'm jealous or anything like that. I want to hate her for giving up. But I guess that for Mae, it wasn't so much giving up, as it was just plain *giving*.

Dill is on the Zamboni sleeping off the pills they gave him when I first hear the crying outside the door. This kid is cold, and angry.

"Does the little guy have a name, at least?" Dill says when he wakes up. He's got a bandage on his face like he just got back from a war.

"I have no idea." I step outside and look out over the balcony for a moment. "Their car's still here. Mae must have left her husband behind."

"Where would she go?"

I imagine Mae floating on her back in some remote cove on the California coast, or maybe up in Maine. "I think she went for a swim."

"What's his name? Kid's got to have a name."

"She told me he don't have one yet."

He shook his head. "Every kid has to have a name."

I think about it for a moment. "Okay. His name's Sam."

"Like, Sam Adams? Or more like Sam Spade?"

"Why does it have to be about anything? I just like Sam. Sam is Sam."

"Maybe you're right," Dill says. "Sam is steady. Sam's your regular bartender. Sam is the auto mechanic you can trust."

"Sam doesn't hold secrets in until he explodes."

Dill leans back. "Yeah," he says. "I've got that cornered."

The kid is in my arms and he won't stop crying. "Maybe he's hungry," I say.

"Rox, we can't keep this kid around. You should give him back."

"Mae left him with us, Dill. And what's this 'we'? You're in no position to tell me what to do," I say. "Mae dropped this kid for a reason. Think about it, Dill."

"That girl isn't old enough to reason, Rox. We can't keep the kid." His voice turns into something different, something you'd find at a traffic stop or at a counter at the DMV: cold, official. "We've got bigger problems than that."

I don't know what he's talking about, but I want to match his voice with mine, since he can't see my eyes or the deep lines in my face. "You forget something, Dill. There's no such thing as '*we*' anymore."

I sit with Sam in my lap and read the Gideon to him out loud. It's the only book we got in the room, but Sam seems to like it. Even without the *Placed by the Gideons* stamp inside the front cover, you can pick out one of their books a mile away: on the first few pages, before you get to any of that *God made heaven and earth* business, they've got this long list of problems, just about any predicament you can find yourself in, from "*Feeling depressed*" all the way to "*Fighting the urge to kill.*" And next to each problem they put the Bible passages you can look up to help you with your problem. I look for "*Being stranded with desperate men,*" but they don't have it. The closest entry I can find is "*Feeling hopeless.*" It says to read Jonah 2:11 and someday when I get that far in this book I'll see what they're talking about.

There's a knock at the door. When someone knocks on your door at a motel it's never good news. A classy hotel, sure, it can be the guy with a bottle of champagne or the maid to do a quick turn-down. But motels are for the folks who want to disappear. I put Sam in his chair on the table and open the door, only a crack. It's Mae's gorilla. Sam has been loud, and I figure the walls were thin.

"You seen my wife?" he says through the crack in the door.

"Nope. Maybe she went out for cigarettes."

"You got my kid in there, don't you? You didn't have a kid when you got here, that's for damn sure." He presses his shoulder on the door, but I hold my ground. "Are you crazy, lady? That's my boy."

He's stronger than me, and he pushes his way into the room. Sam starts crying again, even louder now.

Suddenly, Dill appears behind me, the bandages off now, his eyes a hideous collage of red and black and yellow at the same time, which gives his blind stare the look of the devil. The gorilla and I both freeze.

In Dill's hand we get a glimpse of the largest handgun I have ever seen.

Dill feels for my shoulder and points the gun past it. "Listen, drummer boy, if you don't get the fuck out of here, I'm going to shove this piece up your ass and pull the trigger."

I don't know who Dill scares more, me or the gorilla. We both look at Dill, his arm out straight and his hand wrapped around this gun, dull and black and humongous, pointing more or less in drummer boy's direction.

"You're crazy," drummer boy says, his hands up.

"Get the fuck out, now," Dill says, his hand starting to shake.

The drummer boy backs up and edges out the door. "I'll be back."

I shut it in his face and lock it, pull the chain, then turn back to Dill. "Where did you get that gun? Dill?"

Dill tosses the gun back down on the bed. "Don't worry about that now. Listen, Rox, I have to tell you something."

I read somewhere, maybe it was the *Forum*, they're trying to change the state name from North Dakota to just Dakota—for tourism, so people wouldn't think of it as a place frozen solid five months of the year. Well, they'll have to do more than that to save a place that voted *hoedown* as the state dance. It's just a dumb idea. It's like putting a sign on the toilet that says "*lavatory*" or "*rest room*": no one cares what you call it, they're still going in there to do the same thing. It's like when parents spell out words in front of their kids, as if a six-year-old would never be able to figure out "Let's put the P-O-R-N-O under the S-I-N-K." It's like calling a drunk a dipsomaniac. If you're a drunk, you say "drunk." If you're not a drunk, you end up coming up with words like "alcohol abuser" or "souse," as if to be nice.

People have a problem telling it like it is. I know I do. When Eggs got sent up to James River for waving a gun around in the SuperValu, we should've just sat down with Annie and told it to her face: "Mama, Eggs is in jail. He'll be out in two to four." But Louise and I hedged around for days until finally she got the news from someone she bumped into at the post office.

In my family, it seems early on everybody had to choose which side of the law they're on: my sister, Louise, has spent most of her adult life trying to be a good cop, and Eggs has spent most of his trying to run away from them. As for me, I guess I'm a fence-sitter: I think there should be laws, sure, I just think people make up way too many of them. There's governments, religions, families, husbands, all trying to make up some rule for you to follow. I've never seen myself as someone who could make up the rules; that is, until the weekend at the *Motel de Love*.

This will sound strange, I know, but I'm just going to tell it the way it comes to me: it takes me a while to remember that this blind man with a gun in my motel room is the same man I spent the past two years with.

"Where the hell did you get the gun?" I say. "Where's the keys to the van?"

"We'll be all right," Dill says. He slides the gun under a pillow, like that makes it all better. "I won't let anything happen to you."

"What's going to happen, Dill?"

"This isn't the way I planned it."

"Planned *what*?"

Dill folds his arms, the way he always does when he's about to tell me something I'm not going to like. "Here's the thing: I can't go back home, Roxy."

"What are you talking about? God, I need a drink." Sam won't stop crying, bucking against my arms now.

Dill sighs. "I got into some business again, with some old boys from James River."

"Business, Dill? *Business*? Why don't you call it what it really is for once."

"You know we need the money. Well, things go wrong. Things go wrong, and I end up taking the blame." He throws his hands up in some kind of sad surrender.

"Things always go wrong. You always take the blame." I put the kid back in his car seat and pace a little on the worn carpet. "Now there's people looking for you?"

"Well, for *us*, really. Roxy, I'm sorry. I thought we'd be three states away by now. Like a long vacation, not forever." He touches his fingers to his crusted eyes. "But I'm no good, not like this. Nothing new about the new Dill, I guess, right?"

"You're the old you, Dill. You'll always be the old you. You're the old Dill who drags everybody else down because you're too stupid to know any better. You're the Dill I fucking can't take anymore." I walk around to the head of the bed and grab the gun, rattling it around in my hand. "I'd blow your brains out right here if you had any." I never pointed a gun at anybody before, and just balancing the thing makes me nervous. But goddamn I'm mad.

"Do it," Dill says. "Pull the trigger. Maybe I deserve it. I mean it."

For the first time since I met Dill, I truly believe the words coming out of his mouth.

I think the real reason why I've seen *Officer and a Gentleman* exactly thirteen-and-one-half times—why do only women get this?—is simple: for most of the movie Gere's character, Zack Mayo, is just a big baby: a big, stupid, muscle-headed moron who won't grow up. Why do we always fall for that? He's no spring chicken, either; he's about three or four exit ramps from a midlife crisis, this guy, and the only thing that wakes him up is his best buddy's suicide. Well, that and true love. But mostly the suicide. Let's face it, his clocks are cleaned way before he carries Debra Winger out and that girl starts singing "*Up Where We Belong.*"

I guess at some point we all look for a big baby. Phil Donahue calls them Peter Pans. The problem is when a girl gets older she starts looking for Dr. Peter Pan, MD, an impossible mix, a guy who can take a vacation because it's Thursday and also remind you to file your tax return on time. He's not out there, nowhere up in NoDak, anyway. I know, I've looked. And so we settle, like when your waitress brings a vanilla milkshake instead of strawberry like you ordered, but you don't say anything until the drive home when you finally mumble, "I'll never go *there* again," and that makes it even worse because you know you will. We settle for guys like *Peter Pan, high school dropout,* or *Peter Pan, petty thief,* because we believe that's the best we're ever going to get, the most we're allowed by some screwy divine law, when we could probably do a lot better just by shucking out fifty bucks for a vibrator and a month of basic cable. But then there's love. Love wants you to forget that you will always feel you're giving much more than you ever get. It wants to draw you into the shallow water and drown you.

Love wants to do belly flops for you at midnight in the motel pool.

There are three of them, and they show up around midnight. The drummer boy kept his word about coming back. I guess it doesn't take much to get the jump on a woman with a baby and a blind man, but it seems too easy, really: a few seconds to jimmy the door and before I know it we have three guys on us. Drummer boy has a gun now. I have Sam in my lap, and for once he's pretty quiet. Dill is up on the bed.

"Just give me the boy. Keep still up there, crazy eyes, or this could go off."

I hold on tight to Sam. "Mae didn't want to stay with you. What makes you think Sam does?"

"Who the fuck is Sam? What are you, anyway? A guardian angel or some shit?"

"Why didn't your kid have a name?"

"What are you talking about, lady? Did Mae tell you that? That's my boy. He's got my name all right. Roy Junior."

He gives me a vicious little smile when our eyes meet. I think about Mae and why she'd tell me her child has no name. The answer's standing right in front of me with a gun. Who would want to hang something like this on a little boy? Who wouldn't want to give him a chance at a clean slate?

"Come on, man," one of the other two guys at the door says. "Get the kid and go."

I don't know much about guns, and I probably never will, but Louise told me once that you can tell right off who wants to actually shoot somebody, and who just likes the idea of a gun in their hand. Take Eggs for instance, my little brother. He walked into the SuperValu in Nazareth on a Saturday morning, made it to the space between the fresh bread cart and the deli rack, and then pulled out a gun and waved it in the air. I think he might have said something like, "Where can I find the baked beans?" Some people actually were kind of laughing, and Eggs laughed right along with them. "Baked beans?" he kept saying, while the police were on their way. "Baked beans?" And a couple people kept saying, "Aisle ten." "Baked beans?" "Aisle ten." "*Baked beans?*" "Aisle ten." And everyone laughed a little.

I know Eggs, and he's a mess, but I don't think he'd really aim to shoot anybody. Kind of like Mae's husband: he's standing there holding a gun in his hand, and he wants to talk about some movie. I have Dill pegged into that category, too, along with Eggs and the drummer boy, but it turns out I'm wrong.

The drummer boy comes closer. His two buddies stand by the door, stiff and nervous. "This is some room you picked, lady," drummer boy says.

"I didn't pick it. Dill picked it."

He looks around some more. "Yeah? Where's Annette Funicello?"

"This isn't *Beach Blanket Bingo*. It's *Here to Eternity*. Burt Lancaster," I say.

Drummer boy waves the gun at the walls. "*From Here to Eternity*? One of the greats. Donna Reed made that one. But look at the sky—there's no planes. There's beach, all right, but no fighter planes."

One of the flunkies at the door takes a step outside. "You crazy? Let's *go*."

I have to admit I'm curious. "Fighter planes?"

"Didn't *Here to Eternity* take place during the war? Pearl Harbor? You need less beach bunnies out here and more heavy artillery. Boom. Boom. Boom." He sticks both arms out and starts pumping them back and forth, pistol in his left, like some kind of anti-aircraft gun. "They got it all wrong. If you're going to do something like that, you've got to do it right."

Suddenly, the dim room erupts. Dill had slipped his hand under the pillow without anyone noticing, and he fires three or four times. A bullet catches the drummer boy right in his chest. I see it happen, almost like it's in slow motion. He drops slowly, like a balloon losing its gas. His cronies run out of the room before he hits the floor.

"Oh, God," I say, because it's all I can say. "Oh, God."

I could lie and tell you I don't remember this part so well. You know, say something like, "*It all happened so fast.*" But the truth is, I just don't want to talk about this part. I wish I could forget it altogether. In a day I go from trying to "work things out" in my marriage at a fleabag motel to holding a baby that isn't mine in the middle of a murder scene. Every cop show I've seen makes it look like something you can get over and wash away. Well, that hasn't happened for me, not yet.

I will tell you this: I remember stomping my foot on the floor, as if I was trying to put out a fire in the carpet. My words came out slow.

"What are you doing, shooting?" I say. "You could have hit me, you're fucking blind."

"I can see a little."

"Where are the keys the van?" I say. "I'm out of here."

"On the table, I think. Take me with you," Dill says. "I'll go back to James River for sure. Dammit, help me."

"I'm through helping you, Dill." I look around, figuring out what Sam and I could take and what we could leave behind. What we could do without.

Suddenly his voice hollows out. "Roxy, I'm scared."

"I am, too."

I know what you're going to say. You're going to tell me that I could do something more, that maybe I have a cold heart. Well, I think that's the moment I feel my heart finally beginning to heat up. I'm afraid of my heart boiling over. When I tell Dill I'm scared, I'm telling him the truth.

You're also going to tell me I don't have a clue on what I'm doing, and I don't know even where I'm going when I walk out that door. Well, you just summed up my whole life.

I pick up Sam in his car seat, and I grab enough to fill one of Dill's duffel bags. I take the Gideon out of the drawer and throw it in there, too; I guess I like the idea of someone having to replace the thing. I think about the odds of my father being the one to come and replace it, coming to a place I've already been, instead of it always being the other way around.

Sam and I get into the van and sit a moment in the parking lot, idling, waiting for things to warm up before we head out. We take turns looking at each other. He stares up at me from the open shell of his car seat with eyes I have seen somewhere before. Things are still on the boil, and all we can do is sit a moment and wait.

I don't know what I'm filled with more, love or hate. I guess no one ever stops long enough to try and tell the difference between the two. Things always end up the same, anyway: mixed.

As we slip out of the parking lot and head towards the interstate, we can hear the sirens getting closer.

We stop at a *Gas' n' Sip* to fill up the van and take on the essentials: coffee, Wonder bread, mashed prunes, a carton of GPCs. The frozen midnight air stings my ears as I lean against the back of the van, watching out for state troopers and waiting for our tank to fill. The lot is empty, except for a couple of guys leaning against the ice machine, trading hits off a bottle of Boone's and smoking reds, trying to stay warm. They look right around the age where things seem to change overnight: one day you're young and you stand outside a gas station and people call you a *punk*, a word you wear proudly like a badge, and the next day suddenly you're old and you stand outside a gas station, and from then on people just call you a *bum*, a word you carry like a log.

The two punks stop talking when they notice me staring at them, but after a second or two of meeting my eyes with theirs, they turn away, silent, indignant. I keep looking at them for a few more moments, waiting for the change to happen right before my eyes.

Inside the van, Sam is quiet the whole time, not sleeping really but not awake either, and what I'm really hoping is he's in the middle of his first daydream. I'm hoping he is right in the middle of something so beautiful it might take his breath away.

Before we decide which way to go, we come up with ground rules; we only have time for two of them. Now, I know there are a thousand rules we could come up with, but we're both trying to start over. We're on our own, and both of us are new to this business of making rules. We're going to keep things simple, Sam and me. Our first rule: we would never hold any secrets too powerful to tell. And second, if we come across a woman hitching her way to the ocean, we would stop for her. We'd take her all the way, east or west, until the road ends, with only the ocean left standing in our way. We would take her in.

The Massacre of the Innocents

Summer 1983

His legs let him run a half mile before they remembered they were attached to the body of Anton Rodriguez, the boy who had never come close to passing that fitness test at school, the boy the rest of the tenth grade knew as *Hungry Hungry Hippo*. The cramp in his gut felt like a stab wound, and the four corn dogs, two fried pickles and chocolate whip deluxe he'd just wolfed down at the fair were about to make a repeat appearance. He doubled over on the side of the road, hands on knees. He could hear his brother's Bronco coming down the road, Foghat growling out of the tape deck, the exhaust belching even louder. As the headlights found him in the darkness, Anton tried to straighten up and catch his breath. Normally he couldn't imagine himself running flat-out for anything, even the threat of death, or worse, his father. But this was different.

Somewhere in North Dakota, an elephant was loose.

"Went that way," he said, still breathing hard, pointing into the vast, checkered flatness of barley fields and scrub that rolled south toward the Badlands. "He's got a good head start. Elephants are faster than you think."

Felipe pulled up on the other side of the road and leaned out the window, spitting a soggy meteor of chaw onto the blacktop. He looked over at his brother and laughed. "You get a name, Little Bear? License and registration, at least?" His girlfriend, Ingrid, was riding shotgun and she laughed too.

Ingrid pointed at the paper bag in Anton's hand. "Are those peanuts?"

"Yeah," Anton said, tossing them into the quackgrass. He crossed the road and leaned on the truck. "And a name could be helpful, actually. Elephants are really smart. If we knew his name, maybe we could talk to him or something."

"Yeah, that's what I'm going to do," Felipe said, shaking his head. "Fucking talk to it."

He opened his door to let the boy slide behind him into the back, but Anton was too thick around the middle and got caught between the seat and the door frame. Finally, with a hard shove from Felipe's elbow, he wedged himself free and landed in the backseat, next to a rifle and his brother's battered beer cooler.

Anton gingerly put his hands on the gun, pushing the barrel away. "Is this loaded?"

"That's my official Galilee County Sheriff's Department-issue elephant gun," Felipe said. "It's always loaded." He spat out the window again as he revved the engine and pulled back out onto the empty highway. After a quarter-mile he made a sharp left onto a dirt access road, heading due south. For stretches he turned the headlights off. "Hey, I thought the old man was covering the fairgrounds tonight," he said into the rearview mirror as they bounced along in the darkness. "How come you ain't playing Follow-the-Elephant with him?"

"He left early," Anton said, rubbing his cheek, which was swollen and sore. "He was real angry. I think he was about to shoot one of the fortune-tellers." Anton leaned back into the seat, glad to be off his feet, soles seared inside his Converse. He would have missed the excitement, too, if his stomach hadn't drawn him over to the gauntlet of food stands between the rides and sideshow tents on one side and the animal menagerie on the other. "Some genius parked the cotton candy stand next to the elephant ring," he said, shaking his head.

Even with a temporary fence it wasn't hard for a twelve-foot-tall animal with a trunk to suck up enough spun sugar to put itself into a frenzy. Anton had been deciding whether to spend his last buck on the shooting gallery or a funnel cake when he heard the crash. Folks just stood and stared as this beast the size of a harvester plowed by, feathery strands of pink and blue tangled around its trunk, flattening the ring toss and then steaming out into the parking lot, denting a few parked cars, and then rumbling out of town, heading due south in the faint moonlight toward Route 85.

The boy pressed his face to the window, hoping to catch a glimpse of the magnificent animal rumbling through the carpet of tall barley. He had seen pictures, but this was the first elephant he'd met up close. "You know, this is the first wild elephant in North Dakota history."

"But it's not wild," Ingrid said, smacking her gum. "It's from the county fair."

"I know, but it's wild *now*. I mean, the last elephant walking free around this part of the world was probably some wooly mammoth in the last Ice Age, thousands of years ago."

"You are one weird kid," Ingrid said. "Phil, you sure he's your brother?"

"Half-brothers, really," Felipe said, slowing down as they came to a rise in the road. At the top of the hill they could spot the shadows of some jackrabbits darting out of their way. Felipe cut the engine, and the truck coasted to a stop at the crest. He turned off the radio. "*El Osito* here reads a lot of books. Wants to go to college or something," he said, his voice lower now. He opened his door and stepped out.

"Don't call me that," Anton said, grumbling. "You know I hate that name."

"Osito?" Ingrid said softly, turning around in her seat. They were all whispering now. "That means 'little bear,' right? After your father? I think that's cute."

"Yeah, it can mean little bear," Felipe said from outside. "But in Mexico, it also means 'raccoon.' The old man likes to call him that, on account he eats anything."

Anton yelled this time. "Fuck you!"

Felipe waved his finger, his back still turned as he peered out into the still night sky. "Careful, Little Bear. Long walk back to town. Now make yourself useful and hand me the elephant gun."

The boy grabbed the barrel with both hands and shoved it halfway out the window, surprising Felipe and making him flinch. "You're asking for it, Osito," Felipe hissed, pulling the gun out of Anton's hands and resting it on his shoulder.

"Dark as hell out here tonight," Ingrid said, pushing her hand around the dashboard for Felipe's smokes. "Damn thing could be standing right next to us." She looked through the windshield as soon as she said it; a few jackrabbits had become curious, appearing out of the darkness.

Felipe took aim at the biggest one, lining up the sights on the big gun. After a few seconds he lowered the barrel, his shoulders getting restless. "I don't know why we're out here anyway. State Police will send out a chopper when the sun comes up."

"We're out here because your father told you to," Ingrid said, lighting a cigarette and leaning back in her seat, bare feet propped up on the dash. The smoke draped into the backseat and made Anton cough.

Felipe came back to the truck, ducking his head inside. "What are you saying? I do whatever he tells me?" His voice was booming now, loud enough to scare the rabbits and scatter them into the darkness.

"You're out here, aren't you?" She wouldn't look at him, glancing down at her watch instead. "It's getting late. I told my folks I'd be home from the fair an hour ago."

"Come on, baby. Let's get a drink at the Sticks."

"Did you hear what I said?" she said, her voice even louder than his. "I got work in the morning. And besides, your old man told you to close that place down," she said, sneering at him, almost singing the words. "You'd better do what he tells you."

Anton had heard about the Sticks at school: it was a roadhouse out on the edge of the county with cold beer and a jukebox, which qualified it as a genuine Shangri-La for anyone old enough to drive but young enough to stay clear of the old men who congregated at Nazareth's one legal bar, Andy's Place. The Sticks hadn't been around long; Anton knew enough about his father's business to know that any business opening without the old man's consent would have a short life.

Except for the rumble of the truck as it navigated the dirt roads that carved Galilee County into lonely squares, they sat in silence. Once in a while Felipe would mutter something under his breath.

Anton started to feel sick again, bounced around by the Bronco's unforgiving suspension, but he also felt good: he couldn't remember the last time he'd spent time with his brother. Felipe could be mean—a trait found in the DNA of every older brother—but there were times he'd be the only one to pay Anton any attention at all.

Finally Ingrid broke the silence, sliding around and putting her arm over the seat. She looked over the boy in the backseat, probably for the very first time. "So, you want to go to college?"

"Maybe," Anton said, shrugging. "I want to study natural history. Fossils and stuff."

"Don't let the old man hear you say that," Felipe said, clicking his tongue against his teeth. "Or that fortune-teller won't be the only one to get shot."

"I thought about going to college," Ingrid said, almost to herself.

Felipe waited a few seconds for the punch line. "You?" he said. "College?"

"Don't look so surprised," she said, slapping his forearm. When he laughed, she slid away, her sharp blue eyes simmering. She took a final drag on her smoke and flicked it out Felipe's window, almost hitting his nose before the wind caught it. "I think about a lot of things, you know."

In the back, Anton pressed his cheek to the cool glass of the window, still hoping to be the one to spot the beast: but this was North Dakota, where anyone could get lost quick, even an elephant.

They reached the Sticks a little before midnight. Anton looked through the windshield: from the outside, this certainly didn't look like Shangri-La, only a fat plywood shack painted green, sitting on a few lazy stacks of concrete. The place looked like it would fall apart in a strong breeze. The roof was a mix of tarred wood and tin scraps, and there was only one window, in front next to the door. There were about a half-dozen cars parked out front. Anton could hear the jukebox pumping from inside.

"This is it?" he said, expecting something more from a place older kids at school would talk about in whispers, a place their father would surely burn to the ground if he knew it was still in operation.

"Oh, this is it, all right." Felipe unhooked his badge from his belt and dropped it on the dash. "All right, Little Bear, you keep watch out here for a few. If you see Dumbo drift by, shoot first and ask questions later. Me and Ingrid are going in there and close this illegal speakeasy down," Felipe said, climbing out of the Bronco. He made it halfway across the parking lot before he realized he was alone; he came back and looked at Ingrid through the dirty windshield. "You coming?"

She looked away, staring out her window. "I really got to get home, Phil."

"Are you coming in," he said, slapping both hands down on the hood this time. "Or are you walking home?"

It looked like she wasn't going to budge, but after a few seconds she opened the door, the muffled beat of the music melting her a little. Ingrid slid off her seat but ducked her head back inside for a moment, giving Anton a quick smile. "See ya, Little Bear." Her smile turned back into a scowl as she glared over the hood at her boyfriend. She slammed the door behind her with two hands and all her weight. Then she opened the door, waited a second, and slammed it again. "I'm coming, asshole. You're buying, though."

From the truck, the boy watched them amble toward the door, arms around each other now as they climbed the stoop and went inside. Ingrid's scent lingered in the truck, something like wildflowers.

Alone now, he eased himself out of the truck and stood in the road, still looking at the horizon, his body shivering from the cold air; even in August, nights could get downright chilly out here. Bored, he went back into the truck and pulled out the rifle. He held it against his thighs, feeling the weight in his arms and shoulders. He had seen an old war movie at the Dakota where the soldiers carried their rifles across their shoulders to ford a stream, so he held it like that, the cool metal of the barrel stinging his neck. He walked a few yards down the dirt road and then back again, taking big steps. Then he lifted the gun over his head and held it in his hands again, barrel out now, stock against the soft flesh of his belly. Raising the stock to his shoulder, he lined up the sights, finger on the trigger, scanning left and then right for something on the dim horizon to aim at—a house, a car, a barn, an elephant. There was nothing. He wondered what the chances were that he would see an elephant tonight. Still aiming into the dark, he imagined the elephant lumbering from left to right and pulled the trigger, closing his eyes as he squeezed. His ear was struck by a thunderclap, the recoil kicking his shoulder and pushing his body back, taking his breath away. The gun clattered to the ground. He panicked, turning his head instantly to the roadhouse, wondering what Felipe was going to do to him, or worse, what their father, *El Oso*, would do to him.

But the music was too loud. Anton picked the rifle off the dirt and watched the people inside pass back and forth in the window; it reminded him of the puppet show he had seen at the fairgrounds only an hour before, or the shooting gallery where you pay a quarter for five chances with a warped air gun to win a prize. He lifted the rifle to his shoulder again and aimed at the people passing in the window, his finger hovering around the trigger guard. He could see his brother dancing with his girl in one hand, a beer in the other. He thought he saw some kids in there from school: a couple of football players who picked on him and a girl who had graduated last year with Ingrid who everyone said was a slut.

He wondered how much his life would change if he actually shot someone for real. He had read a book once where a girl in high school gets made fun of by other kids because she has her period in gym class—but she's telekinetic, so she gets her revenge by crashing their cars or electrocuting them at the prom. She blows up a gas station. The girl's mom makes fun of her too, so she kills her by stopping her heart.

Anton had wished for super powers, powers strong enough to destroy a gas station, every time he had to undress for gym class in the cramped locker rooms of Galilee Central School. The other boys would chant "*Hungry Hungry Hippo!*" like the TV commercial and point at his round and hairless body. Soft baby fat still clung to his limbs and his bare skin was mottled, not smooth and fair like his mother's nor brown and leathered like his father's hide.

At the end of the book, the taunted girl dies, but that's only because her mom stabbed her with a kitchen knife. Anton had expected there would be dire consequences for killing so many people, but there weren't any; no police manhunt, no holy curse from above, just a simple stab wound that could have been prevented by not trusting your mother or your father.

Anton thought about his own father. Secretly he wondered whether he hated the old man enough to kill him. Sometimes he would even dream about it.

Severo Rodriguez sat in his pickup and lit another Tiparillo, in honor of the latest doctor to inform him another of his internal organs had turned against him. "Your body's like a clenched fist," this bespectacled boy had said to him with a straight face. "You need to let go a bit, loosen that grip."

Severo was parked on a lonely hill on the edge of the county, a long hump of sour ground dotted with survey flags that would one day be an outlet mall. This was the dreaming left to an old man: people would drive up from Minot or Williston on a Saturday to buy shoes and dress shirts. He had built just about anything worth a damn in this county: the grain elevator, the rec center, the county pool. He built the park on the one lake in the county that wasn't dead with alkali. And he built the new county hospital, so twelve-year-olds with stethoscopes and fancy diplomas could come up from Bismarck and tell him to loosen up. The crook of his arm still itched from the blood they'd drawn. He took a long drag on his cigar and reached for the jar of corn wine on the passenger seat.

Fuck doctors.

There was a morning radio show coming in from Regina on the little Philco he kept on the dash, but he wasn't listening. The sun was coming up. He picked up his binoculars off the passenger seat and scanned the blank horizon.

Fuck elephants, too.

He took another pull of wine, wiping the drops that had seeped into his grey beard with the back of his hand. He was restless, and it wasn't over doctors or this wild elephant business. He'd been sitting there most of the night, running the engine every once in a while to get the heater going; for someone called The Bear, he never had gotten used to the cold, even the faint chill of a late August night. He didn't need an excuse to lose sleep—he often spent the night in his truck, to spare himself the physical pain of undressing and lying down, and the mental pain of lying next to a woman he could not stand—but tonight his mind was filled with something else, something that felt weird and foreign. It was something like fear.

He was thinking about the fortune-teller.

As a young boy, his father had taught him never to believe in anything that didn't come with a clear bill of sale. Growing up in San Antonio, Texas, it was common knowledge that his old man stoked hate for everyone: barflies and teetotalers, slackers and show-offs, dummies and know-it-alls, thieves and martyrs; men, women, babies, geezers, even the dead. But he had reserved the white-hot embers of his rage for anyone fool enough to waste their time with spirits, prayers, and any other magical nonsense.

The old man had lived his whole life as a clenched fist.

Severo could remember walking Guadalupe Street in San Antonio as a little boy with his father. The old man would stop dead on the sidewalk and point out any superstitious fools: the old woman crossing herself as she hurried past the Little Flower cemetery, the kid who would rather cut into traffic than walk under a ladder, the young mother who believed buying some herbs and saying the right words might help her son lose the fear. His father called them all *curanderos*, which was the word for the faith healers, a title of respect, but out on the street his old man would use the word like a sledgehammer.

"*Ese curandero loco!*"

He remembered his father's bullhorn of a laugh, which had never been used in good humor.

"*Mira, mira! Ese curandero loco!*"

Severo took another drink. He remembered priests and nuns crossing to the other side of the street on Sunday just to avoid the old man, a man who'd eventually die far away in North Dakota, digging up sugar beets for three dollars a day like the rest of the *braceros* that came up from Texas back in the 1930s. Severo would have died like that, too, but he'd had other plans. When his father had died in 1938, he was halfway through the State Police academy, not interested in attending the old man's funeral, if there was one at all.

But now he was the old man. *El Oso Viejo*, Felipe called him to his face these days. *El Oso Enfirmizo*. To his face! There was a time when he would have knocked his sons on their ass if they said anything, much less an insult. His wives, too. Now everything in his body was slowly turning sour, even his blood, but that wasn't what was bothering him; in a way, he'd welcome death. That fortune-teller, or whatever it was he claimed to be—magician, swami, complete quack—had made him think about what would come *after* death, and that's what really grated on his mind.

He had been at the fairgrounds the night before, the first night of the county fair, walking around with Osito, his useless son. Severo was there to gloat; over the years he'd turned the old threshing festival—basically an annual hoedown with tractors and beer coolers—into a real county fair, with three days of rides and games and freaks and the last couple years, even animals. The traveling carnival that came into town for the weekend wasn't much more than a mud show, but it did have an elephant. The fair over in Divide County wished they had an elephant. The sheriff over in Williams couldn't even spell elephant.

Walking around the fair, Severo had a big smile on his face, mostly because there was an election coming up. Father and son came upon a small crowd gathered around the entrance of one of the fortune-teller's tents. Among them were two old men of Nazareth, Red Otto and Bill Engvaldson. The tent was painted with glittery stars and comets and had a sign that read "*Melchior the Magnificent—Astrologer to the Crowns of Persia and Mesopotamia—Fortunes Told, Lucky Charms.*"

"Come on, sheriff," Red said, taking a dollar out of his pocket and putting it into the fortune-teller's jar. "You're not afraid of a little hokum, are you?"

Normally Severo would stay clear of such superstitious nonsense, his father's spectre still lingering, but votes were votes, and the election was only a few months off. After Felipe won as sheriff in November, he could officially retire. He could tell everyone to go to hell, even the old men of Nazareth.

Severo ducked into the tent and sat down at the small table, turning down the squelch on his hand radio and dropping it on the thick felt cloth. He took off his wide-brimmed hat and dropped it on the table, too. The crowd closed in behind him, the younger ones giggling amongst themselves. "All right,

Melchior the Magnificent," he said. "Let's make this quick, I've got a lot to do tonight."

The fortune-teller had a gaunt face, his long chin outlined by a pencil-thin moustache and goatee that ended in a sharp point. His head was covered with what looked like a purple turban stuffed underneath a silver crown, encrusted with sparkly jewels. In front of him on the table he had parchments and scrolls laid flat, all with different charts of stars and planets.

"When is your birthday?" he said slowly, not looking up from the table. His hands were folded in front of him.

Severo leaned back in his chair. "Why the hell do you want my birthday?"

Osito had managed to weave through the crowd and stand behind him. "He's an astrologer, Pop. He needs to know your sign to tell your fortune."

"You want to know my sign?" Severo said, shaking his head and slapping the table in mock disbelief. He had plenty of practice milking a moment for an audience. "Hell, where am I, San Francisco?" There were a few titters.

"April twenty-first," Osito said from behind him. "He's an Aries."

Leave it to my useless son to know all about the zodiac sign, Severo thought to himself.

The fortune-teller nodded, then sat deep in his chair and closed his eyes, both hands now raised to his forehead. Opening his eyes, he then looked down at the charts in front of him, slowly moving his head from side to side, as if they were telling him a story. "You are a man of great power," he said, still looking down.

Severo chuckled, looking down at the badge pinned on the front of his hat. "Amazing. No wonder they call you Melchior the Magnificent."

"You are a man of great power," the fortune-teller said again. "People respect you. They fear you."

Severo was quickly becoming bored. "Yeah, yeah—and when my oldest boy takes over he'll be a man of great power, too," he said with a steely smile. "Already know that. I get it. Anything else?" He started to get up.

"I do not see that," the fortune-teller said quickly, almost interrupting him. Then he drew a deep breath and sat silent for a few moments. "Your father worked with his hands. He came from far away."

Severo sat back down in the chair. "Whoa, whoa—back up there, Melchior." He leaned across the table, his voice lowering to a growl. "What do you mean, *you don't see that*?"

The people behind him leaned forward, unable to hear what they were saying.

"I am sorry," the fortune-teller said, pushing back from the table. His eyes darted around like nervous birds. "I am very tired. I must rest."

"You're *tired*." Severo stood, throwing his arms up. "You hear that? He's tired."

"Come on, Pop," Osito said, pulling on his father's arm. "Leave the guy alone."

Severo cocked back with his open hand and smacked the boy hard across the mouth. The boy crumpled into the dirt outside the tent. "Don't ever tell me what to do again," he yelled.

Everyone in the crowd had stepped back, watching with open mouths; all except for Ole Simonson, the oldest man of Nazareth, whose eyes had narrowed.

Severo stood there, uncomfortable under all the stares. He ripped his hat off the table and yelled at Osito again. "Now get up." He took out his wallet and tossed a few dollar bills onto the ground in front of the boy. "Get yourself a treat and then get home."

The crowd dispersed in silence, leaving Osito to get up by himself.

Severo turned back to the fortune-teller. "Now listen close, Melchior, or whatever your name really is: I'm going to be back here tomorrow night. Oh, you bet. I'm going to be back here tomorrow night, and I'm going to put another dollar in this jar, see? And then I'm going to put my hand right here and tell you my birthday. And you're going to do all your stupid astronomy stuff and tell me what I want to know. Understand?"

The fortune-teller sat motionless, sweat beading on his face.

Severo leaned forward, putting one hand on the table, the other on his gun. "I said, do you understand?" Finally, Melchior nodded slowly.

Severo picked up the radio and backed out of the tent. Outside, things looked normal; the boy had disappeared down the midway. Severo started toward the parking lot, his face still sweating into his beard and down into his collar. Behind him, he could hear that fossil Ole Simonson and his cronies still talking to each other in their tight gaggle of craned necks. They must think he was deaf. Severo could hear one of those old crows spit into the ground and whisper, "I'd rather be Rodriguez's pig than his son."

Severo sucked the last life from the Tiparillo and opened the truck door to toss it out.

Fuck the old crows of Nazareth.

A leg had fallen asleep. He opened the door to the truck and planted his feet in the loose dirt outside, gingerly at first, not wanting to break anything. A Mickey Gilley song crackled on the radio. He unzipped and tried to piss, but it burned. He waited, hopping back and forth with the morning chill. After a minute, a lonely dribble of piss trickled into the dirt. He zipped up his trousers and spat into the wet ground.

He wasn't worried about the election; he hadn't worried about an election since 1950. The total population of Galilee County had remained pretty much the same since he had become sheriff thirty-three years before: about a thousand souls, not including livestock and drifters. He had told his son Felipe time and again: you get 150 votes, and it's a landslide. Severo had held this job all those years because he'd been backed by the fancy suits in Bismarck and the old men of Nazareth every four years. And they would back Felipe in November, he was sure of it. He was worried about Felipe, though. He was beginning to believe the boy couldn't be trusted. Twenty-six, tall and handsome like a movie star, and tough—but when it came to doing what was necessary around here, Severo had his doubts. Last night the fortune-teller had dropped a pebble of doubt in his mind. Just twelve hours later, it was now a heavy stone, sitting low in his aching gut.

"Loosen that grip," he said, trying to mimic the doctor's squeaky voice. Severo laughed. "Only when I die." Then he climbed back in the truck and started it up, revving the engine a few times before putting it in gear and rolling back down the hill until the headlights found the access road. He turned north, back towards Nazareth.

Joachim's Tractor & Tire employed three men in the busy summer months; Annie liked to call them her Billy Goats Gruff, due to their ages being spaced perfectly in descending order, and their willingness to pawn off work and blame on whichever of them wasn't in the room. Sven Anderson was sixty; he had worked there ever since the shop opened in a surplus Quonset hut they got from the Air Force. Emile LaCroix was forty; he worked full-time at the shop for the harvest season, then drove a truck in the winter. Lonnie was, well, Lonnie. He didn't know much about engines yet, but it wasn't for lack of enthusiasm. If she didn't pay the kid a dime he'd probably still show up every day; he wore the oil stains on his coveralls like merit badges. She had in fact never once seen him wearing anything but those blue coveralls with the big *Joachim's* logo on the back, even at the movie theater. On the front he'd stitched his name: *Daredevil Lonnie*. He called himself the local daredevil, even though the biggest jump he'd done with his dirt bike so far was Turtledove Creek, which everyone knew was fifteen feet at its widest and just damp dirt most of the year. He'd talk about working up to a jump across the Little Missouri, but Annie hoped it was just talk.

Most days, she liked to pick up coffee and hard rolls for the men on her way to the shop, but that morning she was running late. As she came in, Lonnie was standing in the bay entertaining Sven and Emile with a story about his night, while the older men sat on their stools and drank coffee. As usual, it sounded like a real whopper.

"An elephant?" she said, catching up on the story. "You're having me on."

"As Evel Knievel is my witness," Lonnie said, holding a hand over his heart. "Hell if Daredevil Lonnie didn't see the whole thing, boys, from the top of the Ferris wheel." He was twenty, an age boys could still get away with talking about themselves in the third person. "And would you believe that Rodriguez kid chased the thing all the way out of town, on foot? Funniest shit I've ever seen since that cow got loose in the SuperValu."

Sven sipped his coffee. "Phil Rodriguez did that? I don't believe it. Only thing Phil ran after was poontang." Emile nodded along with him.

"Not Phil—the younger one, the fat one. Kids call him Hippo. Hot damn, I hope someone took pictures. I can see the headline on next week's *Prairie Dog*: '*Hippo Chases Elephant.*'"

"The boy's name is Anton," Annie said with a frown. "You all know that."

Emile finished his coffee and stood up, stretching his thick, stubby legs. "Well, was it a lady elephant? Maybe baby Anton thought it was his mama." He waddled around in a circle on the bay floor with a stupid grin on his face, tongue wagging out. All three men laughed out loud.

"Enough," Annie said. "That ain't funny. Sven, don't you and Emile got a trannie to rebuild?"

"I'm gonna do it," Lonnie said, rubbing his palms together. "Sven says I'm ready."

She looked over at Sven, who gave her a half-hearted shrug in reply. She wasn't against learning experiences, but the eight-speed dual-range transmission on a Ford 4000 was no place for a beginner, especially when it belonged to an old-timer like Bill Engvaldson, who complained even when the work was perfect. "Sven rebuilds the trannie," she said. "You sweep up the shop."

Lonnie folded his arms. "Aw, that's an Eggs job."

"Well, Eggs ain't here yet, so now it's a Lonnie job." She watched the boy grab the push broom off the wall and stand behind it, pushing it only an inch or so at a time. At that rate, he would finish both bays by lunchtime next week. "Almost forgot," she said, her voice now booming for the benefit of the two other men. "You mind telling us who you were on top of the Ferris wheel *with*?"

Sven and Emile looked at each other, then at Lonnie, their faces now sharp with curiosity.

Lonnie pushed the broom harder. "I'm sweeping, boss woman, I'm sweeping."

Annie smiled and nodded her head. "That's what I thought," she mumbled to herself.

She had seen him out a few weeks ago with Phil Rodriguez's girl, which was probably the most dangerous stunt Daredevil

Lonnie had ever attempted. She didn't know Phil all that well, just a quick word now and then at the Rooster, but she did know his father, and that's what really had her worried. Lonnie was too young and too proud to understand how much trouble he'd bring himself by getting anywhere near the bad side of the Old Bear. Severo Rodriguez had been sheriff for thirty-three years now, partly because there had never been a murder recorded in Galilee County during all that time. He kept the peace, which kept the old men around here happy. But he also kept secrets; she would bet the shop on that. There may be no murders recorded around here, but there sure as hell were some accidents, most recently the Old Bear's own brother-in-law, who supposedly drowned in Turtledove Creek last summer when it was usually bone dry.

She told herself she worried too much, that this fear for young Lonnie lodged in the spare bedroom of her mind was just some kind of empty-nest thing, a mother's natural reflex, but she also knew it wouldn't be too much of a stretch to imagine Daredevil Lonnie having himself one of those local accidents.

Annie walked behind the long counter and into her office to check the phone machine for messages. This was all part of her morning ritual now, like brushing her teeth or taking the pills for her hip: she would take in a deep breath, press the rewind button on this contraption, stand over it with her hands in the pockets of her jeans, and hope to hear her daughter's voice. She wasn't quite sure how the thing worked, but it was the one piece of newfangled technology she found useful.

First message: Bill Engvaldson, wondering when he could pick up his tractor. Second message: Bill Engvaldson, wondering if she got the last message wondering when he could pick up his tractor. Third message: parts warehouse in Williston. Fourth message: a woman, a familiar voice—and for a second Annie's hopes spiked; but it was only Betsy, her niece.

"Are you still planning on coming out to see the baby today? I just tried you at home, but you must have just left. Anyway, I hope you do come. Little Jan can't wait to see his Great-Auntie Annie!"

End of messages.

Annie exhaled, easing down into her chair, its little wheels squeaking a bit on the concrete floor. She had forgotten all about promising to visit her new grandnephew. Was it Saturday already? She felt tired, and it wasn't even nine in the morning.

Wasn't Jan a girl's name most of the time?

Sven was leaning on the door frame, his thumbs hooked in the belt loops of his coveralls. He cleared his throat. "Where's young Egbert?" he said in a soft voice.

"We got home late from Minot, thought I'd let him sleep in a bit." She rubbed her eyes and leaned back in the chair. "I wish his parole officer would make the trip up here once in a while."

"Any word from Roxy?"

Annie didn't look up, just shook her head slightly. "You heard the machine, didn't you?" It wasn't a question. This was part of the morning routine as well: Sven standing in the door frame and asking about Roxy, then Annie looking away and telling him no. She wished he'd stop asking altogether. Sven was a good man and an even better mechanic, as good as Joachim ever was, but when it came to things you can't fix with a set of Craftsman tools, he wasn't much use.

He shifted on his feet. "So, I was at Andy's Place last night, drinking a couple beers with some of the boys," he said. By "*boys*" he meant the old men of Nazareth who gathered most nights at the town's one bar, all of them born in Galilee, none of them under sixty-five. They spent their evenings sipping schooners of Miller Lite, trying to remind each other of the old times before they forgot them. Around ten-thirty they would disperse, ready for bed. Sven wasn't one of the boys—he had grown up in Fargo, and he was a youthful fifty-eight—but he was hopeful. "Heard Dill's back at James River again."

"I heard that, too. Some kind of parole violation, right?"

"You could say that," Sven said. "If they get him for manslaughter they'll tack on twenty." He looked at her for some kind of reaction, but there wasn't any. "She's a good girl, Annie. She'll show up."

"Sven—"

He was already backing up. "I know, I know," he said, hands now out of his pockets and waving in the air like he was backing out of a tiger cage. "I got a trannie to rebuild. But if you ever want to talk, you know—"

She pointed out toward the bays. "The Ford, Sven. The Ford. And do me a favor, tell Emile to check the pressure on the air gun. It felt a little weak yesterday." Sven nodded in return, but she had already swiveled her chair away from the desk, gazing out the back window at the tractor graveyard.

Annie was never one to complain; she didn't see that as a virtue, just something left over from her own childhood in a house that somehow made it through the Great Depression in one piece. The last thing she wanted to be was some kind of martyr, with her problems blowing around in public like a stack of loose paper hit with a strong wind. If she did open up to someone, though, she figured it'd make quite a story, something worthy of the afternoon soaps: twenty-five years ago her husband had found God and picked up stakes, leaving her with the repair shop and three young kids, one of whom was now missing, and another out on parole after waving a gun around in the supermarket. Lord knew she'd earned the right to complain, but she didn't want that right. She wondered how much easier this all would be if Joachim had been around the last twenty-five years. The only evidence he'd ever existed was his name on the sign out front and a few scattered memories she kept in her head like frayed Polaroids. Maybe it would've been harder with him here; after all, she had loved the crazy fool, and love never made anything easy.

The carnival had pulled out in the night. Severo idled his pickup for a few minutes at the front gate of the fairgrounds; they were deserted, except for a few pieces of lumber and rope and a dumpster full of trash. The sun was up now, warming the dry air. Flies danced around a few scattered piles of dung; a dog investigated a trampled hoagie.

He had told Felipe to keep an eye on the fairgrounds last night.

"Send a boy to do a man's job," he growled, hands choking the steering wheel until they hurt. Suddenly a jagged bolt of pain shot up from his gut all the way to his jaw; he leaned back, clutching his belly, his breath short and shallow. After a minute the pain ebbed a bit, allowing him to push his hand around the passenger seat in search of his pills. He managed to swallow a few of them, chased with a sip of shine from the fruit jar. Fuck doctors. Fuck useless sons, too, all of them.

He whipped the truck around and headed back out of town, toward the Red Rooster. He was far from hungry but Felipe might be in there, like he was most mornings, killing time while his girlfriend waited tables.

The vehicles in the Rooster's parking lot were all familiar, except one, a black van that had *"passing through"* written all over it. Severo pulled up alongside and turned off his ignition. He sat there for a minute, looking this alien vehicle over. There was an airbrushed painting of a woman in a metal bikini holding a sword and riding some kind of giant lizard. Severo shook his head as he got out and walked up the wooden ramp in front of the café. With the carnival vanished, he was in no mood for another sideshow.

He walked in and dropped his hat on the empty table by the front window. He looked around for Felipe, but there was only Elmer Scobey behind the register and Bill and Red at their usual table by the window. Elmer Scobey owned the place; Bill and Red just acted like they did. In the back were three strangers, obviously the freaks who owned the van outside. He could hear Felipe's little blonde girlfriend in the kitchen, humming something to herself.

"Hey, there's the sheriff himself, ask him," Bill said, his mouth half-full of egg.

"Morning, boys," Severo said, trying to manage a smile. "Ask me what?"

Red tugged his suspenders. "You must've really put the fear of hell into them, huh, sheriff?" Red said, raising a gnarled finger and pointing it out the window toward the fairgrounds. "I mean, you told them fellas to clear out by dawn, was that it?"

"You bet," Severo said, easing into a chair. "You know I don't tolerate any trouble around here. Anyone causes a public disturbance in my county, they pay the consequences."

"Heck, I knew it. Pay up, Bill," Red said, holding his hand out as the other man reached in his overalls pocket and pulled out a loose fold of bills. Red gazed out the window at the empty fairgrounds, shaking his head in disbelief. "You must've scared them half to death, sheriff. Heck, I didn't know you could take down a Ferris wheel that fast. Them fellas disappeared out of thin air like Henry Houdini."

Bill slapped a dollar into the other man's palm. "Fine. But now what do we do tonight, with no fair? Go elephant hunting?"

"You'd need a bigger gun," Red said, blowing on his coffee. "What's playing at the Dakota?"

Ingrid came in from the kitchen. "You got *Indiana Jones* or *Meatballs 2*." She took the carafe from the coffee machine and came over to their table. "Saw the last truck pull out about a half hour ago," she whispered to Severo as she poured his coffee. "Right about the time these yahoos pulled in." She nodded towards the strangers in the corner.

Severo leaned forward and looked them over: they looked hungover. Maybe still drunk. To him, they looked like refugees from some sixties hippie flower-power California love-in. Rock and rollers maybe, judging from the hair and crazy clothes. Or maybe visitors from another planet.

"Hey, honeypie," one of the yahoos called out. "Can I get some more coffee over here, too?"

"Yeah, and your phone number," another blurted out. "He wants to ask you out."

The first one punched his friend's arm. "Dude, shut the fuck up."

"Okay, okay. Probably don't have phones around here, anyway."

"Yeah, they use soup cans and string."

Severo smiled. *Dude.* They called each other dude. He noticed Elmer Scobey get up like he was about to go over there, but Severo put his hand up. Elmer sat back down.

Ingrid went to their table and topped off their mugs. "You want anything else?" she said, already fishing their check from her apron and letting it fall on the table.

They slurped coffee for another minute, then threw some money on the table and headed towards the door. Severo looked them over as they passed by. These punks were lucky Red and Bill were in here; otherwise, he might mistake these three assholes as part of the carnival that just split town, which meant they would have to be questioned down at the jail. A lot.

He met eyes with the lanky one, who stopped short of the door.

"And who are you supposed to be, old timer? Roscoe P. Coltrane?"

The other two hurried their friend out the door, smiling weak apologies.

Severo raised his coffee cup and smiled. "You gentlemen have a safe journey now."

He waited until the old men left the Rooster and drove out of sight before he got up, putting his hat back on. "Tell my son I want to see him," he said to Ingrid. She nodded.

Elmer handed him his hat as he slipped out the door.

There was no hurry. He had watched from the window as the van made a left onto the highway. They were now heading east on a road that had no turnoffs for twenty miles.

Severo eased into his truck, his gut still shredded with pain. He pulled out of the parking lot and rolled towards the highway, turning left. The truck rattled as it picked up speed. He caught up with the van too quickly, it couldn't have been doing more than fifty, so he backed off for a few miles; this sort of thing was better done away from town. After a few more miles he rolled his lights and buzzed the siren a couple of times until the van pulled off onto the shoulder.

Dude.

Severo stepped out onto the blacktop, pulling the strap off his sidearm as he walked slowly to the van. This was going to be easier than he'd thought; he could smell the pungent aroma of weed wafting out of the driver's window. The only thing that would make this situation better was if one of them drew a gun. A knife, maybe. But looking in on the two sitting in the front of the van, he decided they weren't the type.

"License and registration," he said to the driver. "Now."

The skinny one with the long black hair was driving; the short one with the tea shades and thick moustache was in the passenger seat, his eyes wide with fear. The third one was poking his head over a seat from the back of the van; he looked simply wasted. Severo was a man who'd worn the same tan pants, shirt and hat for the past thirty-three years; to him they looked like castaways from a gay pirate ship.

He took a step back from the window as he examined the Montana license. Then he stuffed the documents in his shirt pocket and came back, resting his arm on the windshield as he looked these three over again. "Who are you guys supposed to be, Sonny and Cher?"

Sonny spoke up with a nervous smile. "We play hard rock, some metal," he said. "Kind of like Van Halen. You know Van Halen?"

"Is that a moving company?" Severo was enjoying himself now. "You sure don't look like furniture movers to me." He looked up and down the highway, which was an empty black line in either direction. "All right, everybody out," he said, pointing to the other side of the road. "Go sit on the shoulder."

The three young men grumbled but did what he told them, clambering out and sitting down on the side of the road, shielding their eyes from the warm sun.

Severo started to snoop inside the front of the vehicle. He poked his head under the driver's seat and—bingo—there was a plastic baggie shoved up in there, wrapped around a hash pipe, the bud still smoking. He pulled it out and turned around, holding it up high. "You—Cher," he said. "You own this vehicle?"

The kid looked at the ground. "You got my registration in your hand, don't you?"

"You should be happy I found this little bag of weed," he said, clicking his tongue. "Saves me the trouble of planting something a lot worse."

Sonny held his hands out. "Look, sheriff, can't we take care of this here?"

Severo smiled. He stuffed the baggie in his shirt pocket. "Whatever do you mean, Sonny?"

"I mean, you must be a busy man, right? And we've got a gig tonight in Grand Forks. Maybe we could just take care of this here?"

Severo nodded his head. "Hot day today," he said. "Old vans like the one you got, they sure do overheat easy." He walked to the back of his truck and opened the work box, rummaging his hand inside. "You know, Sonny, you're right: I *am* a busy man. But never too busy to help some good folks stranded on the side of the road." He came back with one of the fruit jars, unscrewing the lid.

"Stranded?" Cher said, squinting in the sun. "What the fuck you talking about, old man?"

"Yeah, we get people breaking down on this road all the time. You bet. Why, just last month we had this van full of young punks, a lot like you actually, and the damn thing just all of a sudden overheated and the engine caught fire, can you believe it? When it was over, we had to put the thing on a flatbed. Couldn't even tow it, on account of the tires melting. Now that's *hot*," he said. He bent down and ripped the bandana off Cher's head, splashed it with some of the barley wine, and then stuck it halfway into the jar, screwing down the lid tight over it. "But that's a NoDak summer for you, hot and dry right up until that first snow."

Cher put his hands on the ground, ready to spring up.

"I wouldn't get up if I were you," Severo said. "Your microbus looks like it could catch fire any second." He was trying to remember where he'd left his lighter when he heard the exhaust of Felipe's truck long before it appeared on the horizon, rumbling towards them from town. He was coming at his usual speed, which was about a hundred miles an hour.

Felipe rolled up behind his father's pickup and hopped out, putting on his sunglasses and standing in the road, thumbs hooked under the thick leather of his gun belt as he took in the situation. He looked at the three boys on the roadside, then at the firebomb balancing in his father's hand. Calmly, he spat on the hot asphalt, clearing his throat. "What are we doing here, Oso Viejo?"

"Helping these boys out," Severo said. "This here is Sonny. That one's Cher. I don't got a name for the other one yet."

Felipe looked away. "You got anything on these boys, or is this another elephant hunt?"

"I got a bag of weed and a pipe," he said. "And I don't have to answer questions from you, boy. Last I checked, I was sheriff around here."

"Not for long," Felipe said, pushing his shades up on his nose.

"You were supposed to hang around the fairgrounds last night, make sure we still had a county fair in the morning."

"Yeah, well," Felipe said, looking away. "I was busy."

"You were out at the Sticks, weren't you? You and the little blonde bimbo," Severo said. "I told you to close that place down."

"Her name is Ingrid. And I will, soon as I get tired of putting money in the jukebox. It's a good place. Back in your day they'd call it a speakeasy."

"There's not going to be any illegal roadhouses in my county."

"You don't seem to have a problem with illegal *stills* in your county," Felipe said, pointing to the jar in Severo's hand. "Like the one in Red Otto's hay barn. And besides, come November, this is *my* county, ain't it?"

"You're an insolent little shit," Severo said. "You'd better be careful." He pictured taking a few jars of barley wine out to the Sticks and burning the whole place to the ground. With any luck, he thought, all the young assholes in Galilee County would be inside—Felipe included. He had another son, after all.

Severo would go up there tonight and drag Osito along with him, the way his own father had dragged him up and down Guadalupe Street back in San Antonio. The boy would have to learn how to be a man, whether he wanted to or not.

Severo smiled over at his deputy, the remnants of jagged yellow teeth sticking out of his black gums like an abandoned graveyard. "Now, I want you to take these assholes back to town and lock them up for possession. And drop by Annie's on the way. Let her know we got another vehicle caught fire on the highway."

Felipe shook his head and laughed. "This is your mess, old man. Not mine."

"I'm giving you an order, boy," Severo growled. "Now, what are you going to do?"

Felipe kept shaking his head as headed back to his truck. "I hope you have fun with Sonny and Cher."

Severo grumbled as he watched the Bronco turn around and head back to Nazareth.

Annie didn't want to visit Betsy and the baby, but she found herself driving over anyway. It wasn't that she didn't like her niece—Betsy was a girl with a good heart, one who had married too young, to a man twice her age—it was just Annie was tired of hearing about The Miracle Baby. Every time she came over here it felt more like a carnival show than a family visit. *Come one, come all! Step right up and see The Miracle Baby! See the baby who cured his own father's stroke just by coming out of the womb! Witness the child who overcame pneumonia, whooping cough, and beriberi and never once cried! View the baby who could already fingerpaint like Matisse!* This time, Betsy would probably try to convince her that Jan was now on the verge of solving the African hunger crisis from his crib.

"Let him solve how to make a decent cup of coffee," Annie said out loud as she pulled onto the gravel track that wound up to the house. "Because his mother sure as hell can't."

She knew she shouldn't be so hard on Betsy. Here was a girl whose one goal in life had been to be a mother, but after marrying old Zeke the preacher, she'd found out she couldn't have kids. She had gone to every ob-gyn in North Dakota and one over in Minneapolis, and they all resisted saying the same word: "barren." But the girl had never given up hope. Nothing else had mattered; she'd prayed, she'd gained weight, she'd lost weight, she'd read every book she could find, she and Zeke had sex just about as many times as the old goat could get it up, and sure enough, about a year-and-a-half ago, she'd been pregnant. Yes, the girl definitely had gumption. Maybe Annie was a tiny bit jealous; after all, Roxy and Betsy had grown up as little girls together, and she couldn't help but wish a little bit of Betsy's spirit would have rubbed off on her own daughter.

Annie walked up to the trailer and rapped on the screen. Standing there, she made herself a bet: every time Betsy said the word "*miracle*," she would allow herself one Milky Way bar when she got back to town.

Today, everybody wins.

Betsy opened the screen door and clasped her hands together. "Aunt Annie!" she said with elegance and surprise, as if horse-drawn carriages had been dropping off guests in the driveway all morning. "I'm so happy you came over. Little Jan is sleeping, but you want to take a quick peek in on him?"

"Wouldn't miss it for the world," Annie said. "Where's Zeke today?"

"Out doing the Lord's work, you know." She led Annie back to the bedroom, padding silently on the thick carpet with pink house shoes. The crib was wedged in the cramped space between the bed and the door. The shades were drawn, making the room dark. "There he is," Betsy whispered. She took a deep breath and let it out. "Isn't he a little miracle?"

"That's one," Annie said to herself, a little too loud.

Betsy had a confused look. "One what?"

Annie pointed to the crib. "That's one little miracle, all right."

Betsy smiled. "Did I tell you about how he cured Zeke's stroke when he was born?"

"Honey, I was in the room when it happened."

She wasn't going to remind her niece how he'd gotten the stroke: Betsy had come home one day and told him she was pregnant. The man stopped breathing right then and there, keeling over on the kitchen table. The doctor had guessed the sudden shock was too much for a part of his brain called Broca's area; he couldn't speak at all after that. That is, until the day Jan was born. Annie remembered it very clearly: every aunt, uncle and distant cousin of Betsy's had stood around her hospital bed, drinking Cold Duck from Dixie cups and wondering what to name the boy. Betsy had been bent on naming him Jan, which to everyone else came out of the blue. Her mother, Annie's sister, wouldn't hear of it. "You should at least name him after the father. Or pick an uncle. In America, Jan's a girl's name."

Old Zeke, who had been sitting in a chair in the corner of the room the whole time, stood up and slammed his hand against the wall. Everyone had stopped talking and turned around. His mouth was in a snarl, his lip curled like a wave about to crash. He wanted to yell something, but couldn't even manage a whisper. So he took the pen off the chart at the foot of the bed and wrote in big, crazy letters on the palm of his hand: *HIS NAME IS JAN.*

And that had been that. By that evening, Zeke's voice had come fully back.

Betsy led her back to the living room. "You know, he called everyone we knew that night, he was so excited. He'd even dial random numbers on the telephone just to talk to people."

"I know. He called my house three times, reading words out of the dictionary." Annie dropped into the easy chair as Betsy went to the kitchen and poured the coffee.

Annie looked around the place; it was immaculate as usual, except for a few stray toys scattered on the floor. Most of the furniture was on permanent loan from family; Annie herself had volunteered the couch, blender, and this particular Lazy Boy, which she had missed more than she would let on. She had bought another as a replacement, the same exact model, but somehow it wasn't the same. This one had better back support, and besides, it had been a present from Joachim; the only other things she'd held onto were two daughters and a son.

Betsy came back in balancing two steaming mugs and a bowl of Oreos. She handed Annie one of the mugs and placed the bowl gently on the coffee table. "I'm ashamed to say these things are my vice, ever since I was pregnant," she said, taking a cookie from the bowl and flopping on the couch, her legs tucked underneath her. "I'm lucky little Jan loves them, too."

Annie dunked a cookie into her mug. "How did you set your heart on the name Jan, anyway?"

Betsy looked surprised. "He's named after Jan-Michael Vincent, of course."

"Of course," Annie said. She sipped her coffee, then put it down. "Who's that again?"

Betsy laughed, rolling her eyes. "He's only the best actor in the *world*."

"Better than Broderick Crawford?"

"Who's that?"

Annie smiled. "Never mind." She grabbed another cookie and popped it in her mouth.

For some reason, Betsy wouldn't stop fidgeting. She seemed nervous about something. "Are you sure you wouldn't want something stronger? Zeke keeps a bottle of whiskey around here someplace."

"Thanks, but I got to get back to work." Annie was about to push herself out of her chair when Betsy leaned over and put a hand on her arm. "What's the matter, girl? You're trying hard not to tell me something. Is it Zeke? The baby?"

Betsy bit her lip. "I heard from Roxy yesterday."

Suddenly, Annie found it hard to move, and in that split second she was convinced she was now the second person who'd been hit with a stroke in this very chair, thanks to Betsy's knack for delivering news. After a few seconds though, her muscles started to loosen again. "Is she all right? Where is she?" Her skin felt hot and sweaty, the Oreos in her stomach now rough stones. "Where did she call from?"

Betsy stood up and circled the living room with her hands behind her back, reminding Annie of those TV movies where people with funny accents solve crimes. "Someplace called Cairo, Illinois," Betsy said, wringing her hands together as she walked back and forth. "I'm not even supposed to say that much. I looked it up at the library: it's about a hundred miles south of Chicago. Only she says they pronounce it 'Kay-ro.' You know, like the corn syrup?"

"I don't care how they pronounce it. What the hell is she doing there?"

"I guess that's as far as she got. She said to tell you she's fine, she's happy. She wanted to call you, but she wasn't sure if the police were still after her or not. And there's something else," she said, biting her lip again.

"Damn it, girl, every time you bite your lip you give me a heart attack. I'm too old for this. Just tell me."

Betsy took a deep breath. "She's got a baby," she said. "A little boy."

Annie's eyes got big. "You know damn well Roxy can't have a baby," she said.

Betsy shrugged. "Miracles happen, Aunt Annie."

"Miracle my ass," Annie said, taking her cup off the table and draining it in one gulp. "Where's that whiskey?"

An hour later, after she'd made Betsy repeat every detail at least five or six times, Annie drove slowly back to town, drifting over the center line a few times, the back of her hand catching the warm breeze. A baby? Could it be true? If it was, she was willing to put some faith in miracles. Right then, she'd be willing to put faith in just about anything.

She felt the warmth of the whiskey in the back of her throat. Wild Turkey on ice, now *that* she could accept as a miracle.

She tried to picture Roxy happy and with a baby, but it was difficult; she tried to picture Roxy just happy, but that was almost as hard. But that's exactly what Betsy had told her: *she's happy*. The girl had had such a rough life already, and she was just thirty-one.

Annie's afternoon buzz vanished as soon as she pulled off the highway and headed toward Nazareth: she saw Severo Rodriguez's pickup parked in front of the shop. What did the Old Bear want? As she pulled her truck alongside in the parking lot, she could see him inside the bays, talking to Lonnie and Eggs. Maybe it was the whiskey or the news about Roxy—probably both—but Annie didn't feel much like dealing with Severo today. She definitely didn't want him anywhere near her son.

"Anything I can help you with, sheriff?"

"A van caught fire out on the highway, about ten miles east of town," he said, twirling his sunglasses on his finger. "Need you to send the wrecker and fetch it."

She nodded. "Lonnie, you and Egbert head out there, okay?" Lonnie jogged back to the office to get the keys. Eggs stood there, folding and then unfolding his arms, unsure what to do next. "Honey, you go with Lonnie," she said to her son. Eggs nodded with a vacant smile.

Severo put his sunglasses back on. "As long as I'm here, let me ask you," he said. "You haven't heard from that daughter of yours, have you, Annie?"

Annie folded her arms, her eyes squinting in the afternoon sunlight. "Louise? Sure, she comes around all the time. You can't miss her. She's the state trooper who hates corrupt local officials."

Severo smiled, rubbing his cheek as if salving a wound. "Not that daughter. I meant the drunk whore," he said. "Not the bull dyke." Then he nodded toward Eggs. "But look on the bright side, Annie, at least they're not all retarded."

Lonnie came up behind her. "Hey, you can't talk to her like that."

Annie put an arm across his chest, pushing him back. "Lonnie, get going."

The boy stood there for a few moments, his arms tensed, frightened from locking eyes with the old man but reluctant to back down at the same time. Finally he took a few steps back, pulling the wrecker keys out of his pocket. "Come on, Eggs," he said, too loud. "We got a job to do."

They went out the back door. Annie could hear the wrecker's diesel engine cough to life and turn over.

She kept staring at the old man; he looked like he was enjoying the moment. Unlike Lonnie, she was too old to be frightened of the Bear, but that didn't mean he wasn't dangerous.

Severo spat on her concrete floor. "Now, I know the State Police aren't looking at her anymore, but that don't mean

I'm not. We don't want any bad apples coming back and hanging around the tree. Girl like that—well, sooner or later she's going to come back, when she runs out of money, or men, or both. So do yourself a favor, Annie. When she does show up in Nazareth, she better come find me," he said, turning back to his truck. "Or else I'm going to come find her. I hope you tell her that."

"You go to hell," she said.

"Oh, any day now," he said, tipping his hat. "Any day."

Then he slipped into his truck and drove off, kicking up gravel and dust, which swirled around Annie as she stood there, alone.

After dinner, Anton climbed the stairs and went into his room, closing the door behind him. It had become his ritual now, escaping upstairs before his father came home; he'd lie belly-down on his bed to read from his stack of library books or play Atari. Once in a while his mother would stick her head in the door to check on him, but most nights he would be left alone until morning. He couldn't remember the last time the old man had actually made it to the top of the stairs; usually the Old Bear would sleep in his truck or slumped across the sofa.

It was around ten when Anton heard his door open. He rolled onto his side and turned to see his father standing in the doorway, looking around the room like he'd just found a new part of the house. The old man belched, the sour mixture of tobacco and barley wine wafting across the room.

"What are you doing in here?" his father asked.

"Playing Atari," Anton said. "Pitfall."

"Well, get your shoes on. You're coming out with me tonight."

Anton lay motionless, his mouth open. He wasn't sure what his father meant.

"Did you hear me, Osito? It's about time you made yourself useful. Get your ass out to the truck." With that, his father turned and walked out of the room.

Anton could hear the old man lumber down the creaky stairs and out the front door. There was an odd feeling of excitement mixed with fear; his father had never asked him to come out with him at all, much less at night this late. It had to be the elephant—Anton was hoping they'd finally found the elephant somewhere out in the wilderness. He grabbed his sneakers off the floor and slipped them on, laces loose and flopping as he ran down the stairs. He rushed outside into the cool night air, his lungs already running short of breath, his legs trying to catch up with the excitement flushed in his face.

The Flight Into Egypt

Autumn 1983

Last winter there had been dreams of Florida, maybe even Mexico. But when Roxy came out of an IGA somewhere in southern Illinois that January, Sam slung in one arm and a paper sack in the other, she saw a police cruiser in the parking lot stopped behind the van, lights silently turning. They must have run the out-of-state tags and not liked what they found; she had overheard some truckers in an Iowa Kum & Go talking about the cops nowadays, how they had radar, lasers, helicopters, spy cameras. Even the county mounties had computers that knew everything about you. All they had to do was look.

She fought the urge to slip away through an alley or back into the store; she knew from experience small towns never had enough places to hide. Their best chance was to put on a dumb smile and amble right past like they lived here; she hoped they could pass for Illinois, whatever that meant. It would help if she knew the name of the town. Probably Cornville. Cornburg. Corn City. Everything in this part of the country was corn.

Roxy passed from a distance in the parking lot. She saw a sheriff's deputy behind the van having trouble pulling the flashlight from his belt. He was a lumpy guy in his twenties, his thick eyeglasses frosted over at the edges with the cold.

When he saw Roxy out of the corner of his eye, he turned around and smiled at Sam. He glanced at the grocery bag and rapped the back window of the van lightly with his knuckle. "Ma'am, you didn't see who owns this vehicle, did you?"

"No, sir," she said cheerily, with a face that suggested they might be old friends. It was easier than she'd thought; but then again, she had made her living as a waitress. She stopped to face him, relaxing her shoulders, hoping the image she projected said something like "I am a lifetime resident of beautiful Illinois, and I don't appreciate it when strangers come from out of state and cause trouble." She looked down at the van's mangled license plate, hanging off the back bumper like a sad tail. "They're from North Dakota? Hell, ain't that a crime in itself?"

Okay, she thought, that might have been too much.

The cop chuckled. "You may be right about that." He looked down at Sam again and made a goo-goo face.

The boy smiled right back; he was already getting good at being an outlaw. There had been some close calls the last couple weeks since they'd escaped North Dakota, but she figured that was part of the deal when you're the wife of an ex-con driving a stolen van with a stolen baby and no driver's license. Scratch that: wife of a con. Last time she had called her cousin, she'd heard Dill was already headed back to James River. At least he could see now.

With any luck, soon she'd be the ex-wife of a con. On her list of plusses and minuses for Mexico, *plus #7* had been the promise of the fifty-dollar divorce.

The deputy turned back to the van. "You two have a nice day."

"You too," she said, producing a warm smile. "See you in church." That was definitely too much. But he didn't seem to care; he was too busy wrestling with the flashlight again.

She reached the sidewalk and started down the street, moving swiftly but hopefully not swift enough to appear desperate. She was glad she had locked the doors on the van; as soon as T. J. Hooker back there saw the baby seat and Pampers, he might put two and two together.

Roxy crossed the empty street and waved a hasty good-bye to the van. As she turned a corner, she said good-bye to Florida and Mexico. They didn't have enough money left to get out of the state, much less the country. If the police were really looking for her, they'd spot the Mexico list on the front seat and put someone at the local train and bus stations. Or maybe she'd get lucky, and they'd just start looking for her way down on the streets of El Paso. But she doubted it.

Two more blocks of houses and she came to the single-lane highway that ran through the middle of town. A light snow began to fall. Sam kept silent, looking up at her with his big blue eyes. "You know, I'd feel better if you started bawling your eyes out," she said. At least then they could be miserable together. The kid had to be hungry. "You're a lot better at this than I am," she said as they started south down the highway. It was a Saturday afternoon with about an hour of daylight left, and traffic was sparse.

She kept looking over her shoulder. Her feet hurt and both arms were pretty much numb from holding up that much weight so long. She wasn't ready to admit it out loud, but more than anything she just wanted to go home, back to Annie's house in Nazareth. She wanted to fall into Annie's favorite chair with Sam in her lap so they could both sleep for a month. But that was probably as much a farfetched dream as Mexico right now; her cousin Betsy said the Old Bear was looking for her—snooping around Annie's shop, asking a lot of questions.

There was only one way out of this town. She stopped and dropped the bag on the pavement. Then she took a deep breath and turned to face oncoming traffic, slowly putting out her thumb. Sam coughed; when she looked down there was a worried look on his face. "I know," she said, holding him tighter. "I know." The kid had a point: what if a cop came by? What if they got picked up by some psycho-killer?

A few minutes passed before a white pickup truck pulled over on the shoulder, *Davidson Carpentry* printed on the door. It had a big cab with a backseat and a shiny toolbox in the bed. The driver was a burly guy with a worn John Deere ball cap on his head and sawdust in his scraggled beard; he leaned over and rolled down the passenger window. "You folks all right?"

Well, she thought, if he was a psycho-killer, at least he had a steady job.

"Car trouble," she said, picking up the groceries. She hoisted herself and Sam into the big truck and closed the door; only later would she marvel at the super-human strength it takes to do all that at once. The cab was warm and the upholstery had that new smell of vinyl. There was a hula girl glued to the dash, the girl's head mysteriously missing. The radio was playing some upbeat rocker by Springsteen she hadn't heard before; must have a new album out. She tucked the grocery bag down under her feet. "Thanks for stopping. Had to get some food before the boy starved to death."

"Not a problem," he said, checking his mirror before steering back onto the highway. "That's got to be a state law, anyway: stop for stranded women holding babies in the snow." He took a sip from a mug of coffee he had balanced on the dashboard as the truck picked up a little speed. "Well, maybe in this state. Where I come from, I'm not so sure."

Her stomach growled. That coffee smelled good. "Where you from?"

"North Dakota," he said with an embarrassed laugh. "You ever driven through North Dakota?"

She froze in her seat. This was turning out to be one fucked-up day. "No, never," she said. "That's Canada, right?"

"Yeah, some days," he said. "Haven't been back in a few years myself, but I'm guessing the roads are just as lonely and crazy as ever. Any state that gives you a driver's license at age fourteen is bound to have problems, right?" He looked over for a reaction, but Roxy wasn't saying anything. He took another sip of coffee. "You lived here long?"

She started to panic: the last thing she wanted was to answer questions, even if the guy was just being nice. "I—I'm a lifetime resident of Illinois," she blurted. "And I don't appreciate strangers coming in and causing trouble."

There was a long pause. "Okay, then," he said finally, scratching at the tangled brown hair under his cap. Springsteen had given way to commercials for farm equipment and a local pizza parlor, so he turned the radio down. The diesel engine chugged patiently beneath their feet. He stole a glance at Sam, making the same goo-goo face as the cop.

What was it about grown men and the fucking goo-goo face?

"Well, you got a great-looking kid there. I got a couple of my own, bit older than yours though."

Roxy tried to act casual as she turned to look out the back window at the empty road behind them. "Two boys?"

"Boy and a girl."

She shifted in her seat. "Are you really from North Dakota?"

"You bet. Left tackle on the Fargo South football team, about a million years ago. Why?"

She closed her eyes for a second; any longer and she might fall asleep. "Sorry," she said. "Just seemed unlikely, is all."

She took a deep breath and let it out, cursing herself for being so paranoid. This guy was all right, he didn't deserve the drama. Sadly, he was already the closest thing she had to a friend in this state, psycho-killer or not.

Roxy sagged against the door and watched the town disappear in the rearview. She was tired enough to start taking chances. But she felt more than tired; she needed repairs, as if parts of her body were about to fall off without notice. "I'm having a really bad day."

"I know what you mean," he said. "Hey, I know a good mechanic if you need one. He's got a wrecker, and his shop's not too far—about halfway between here and Cairo." He slowed down a little; there was a crossroads coming up. "Where'd you leave your car?"

She sat up and looked over at him, trying to read his eyes in the dim light. "Florida."

Now it was September, and Joe Davidson was sitting on the back porch, his little girl Lydia parked next to him on the bench as she attacked a spiral notebook with crayons. It was a good day for yard work, warm and dry, and he knew there was plenty to do around the house—he was a single father with two young kids, there was always something to do—but he'd been distracted all day, his mind somewhere else.

He was deciding whether or not to tell Roxy about the dream.

The house had a long backyard with a lone sycamore entrenched at the far end, a huge tree probably older than Cairo itself. Beyond that a fallow cornfield stretched all the way to the Ohio River. In the summertime, his son Jimmy would climb through the sycamore's thick brown branches or hide out in its hollow; the space was wide enough to hold a washing machine. Its fat oval leaves had just started to turn; in a few weeks, Joe would rake them all up into a pile, and the boy and his best friend, Darvell, would spend hours trying backward pikes and jackknifes and belly flops, Lydia getting lost in the mound like a mole. Lately she'd ask him to hoist her up into the hollow so she could pretend it was the spaceship from *Pigs in Space*. The girl was crazy about Muppets. For some reason, Joe always got the thankless role of the old scientist, Dr. Strangepork, and since he was too big to climb inside the tree, he was usually relegated to spacewalks and lookout duty. And going back to the house on a Ho Ho run.

"Daddy," Lydia said, tugging on his jacket as they sat on the bench. "Guess what this is."

He didn't have to look down at the notebook; so far, he'd already seen eleven caterpillars that day. But he turned and looked anyway, furrowing his brow. "Is that a caterpillar?"

She nodded happily.

"Can I just say that is the best caterpillar I've seen all day?"

She turned the page over to start number thirteen. "You always say that."

Last week it was frogs. Every day when he'd pick her up after preschool, she asked if they could go down to the levee and listen to the river frogs chirp at one another into the dusk.

This week it was caterpillars, and he knew it was only a matter of time before she'd head back to the sycamore to count the caterpillars crawling around its huge trunk. They liked to come out right before dusk. Lydia would stick her face right up to the little critters, almost touching them with her nose. Probably had even licked a few. Pretty much every night, two or three of them would mysteriously appear on the dinner table.

He looked on the bright side: two weeks ago, it had been polar bears.

"Can we have pizza tonight?" she said, looking over the crayon selection she had laid out between them. Burnt sienna seemed to be the color of choice this time around.

"Sam and his mom are coming over tonight, Queen," he said. "I thought we'd cook something nice for them. Maybe crack one of those cookbooks we've got above the sink. What do you think?"

She stopped drawing and looked up at him. "I think we should get pizza tonight," she said with a slow, deliberate voice.

For a moment, Joe felt like the four-year-old. "You like little Sam and his mom, right?"

Lydia thought about it, then nodded. "You call her Rocky," she said. "Is that her name?"

"Yeah, sort of. We'll go pick them up in a little while."

He'd called her Rocky Balboa ever since they had caught *Rocky III* at the drive-in that summer. He figured if anyone deserved a statue based on toughness, it was her. She didn't seem to mind, mostly since it gave Joe an excuse to do his Mr. T impression in front of Sam; it was god-awful, but for some reason it was the only sure-fire way to get the kid to stop crying these days, with his molars finally coming in.

He would definitely *not* mention the dream. After all, it'd taken this long just for her to agree to stay over for the night. Conditions did look favorable: James was doing a sleepover at Darvell's house to play Atari or whatever else eight-year-olds did on a Saturday night these days. And for all her energy, Lydia was usually out for good by eight o'clock, nine at the latest.

James's voice squeaked from the kitchen window behind them. "Dad, Mr. Barnett's here."

"Ask him to come round back, okay?"

Will Barnett was a deputy sheriff for Alexander County, and his son, Darvell, was in the same homeroom with James, both prisoners of some old battle-axe named Mrs. Spitznagel who had probably taught school in Cairo, Illinois since the days of the original pharaohs.

"Hey, Joe," Will said, putting one foot up on the porch. He was a compact man about Joe's age, maybe a few years younger, white hairs betraying an athlete's frame. He looked different without his sheriff's uniform, maybe more relaxed. "Queen, how are you today?"

She smiled and held up the open notebook with both hands.

Will leaned closer to the picture. "Hey, that's really good. Subway train, right?"

Joe put a hand over his mouth and pretended to cough. "*Caterpillar.*"

Will rubbed his chin. "What was I thinking? You know, that's the best caterpillar I've seen all day."

Lydia looked at both men, suspecting some kind of compliment conspiracy.

"Can we go now?" James whined from the window. Darvell's head was poking out of the window now, too; a two-headed monster of early adolescence.

Joe suspected there was more than just childhood impatience behind his son's carping; the boy was old enough to remember his mother, and he wasn't warming up to the idea of another woman in the house. At some point, they'd have a talk, but it'd wait for now.

"Don't forget your new games," Joe said to his son. "I think they're on the TV. Missile Invaders or Space Command or whatever you call them."

"Missile Command and Space Invaders," James corrected, not looking at his father. "Those are *old* games. You mix up the names on purpose."

Joe shrugged. "Could be."

"Man oh man," Will said. "Remember when we were kids? Kick the can?"

"Yeah—find a couple of sticks on the ground, and you've got enough to play army. Now they sit in front of the TV screen all day and push a button."

"We don't just play video games," Darvell said. "We do other stuff, too."

Will turned and looked up at his son, arms folded across his chest. "Like what?"

"Lots of stuff," the boy answered quickly, but there was a long pause before he could come up with something. "We watch *Dukes of Hazzard*." The two boys nodded to one another approvingly, their thick plastic eyeglasses moving up and down almost in concert. "And I got that new chemistry set. We could make a volcano explode or something."

Will smiled painfully. "Thanks. I feel a lot better now."

"We got homework, too," Jimmy added. "We're doing a diorama of the Roman Empire." With that, both boys disappeared into the house, the window banging shut behind them.

Joe put a heavy hand on Will's shoulder. "Sorry, man," he said with a sad note of sympathy, like there had just been a death in the family. "You get diorama duty."

"Me? No, I'm lucky. I'm out on patrol tonight. Cheryl's the one on diorama duty."

"Well, tell her sorry for me," Joe said. "Next weekend I'll probably get school play."

"Halloween ain't so far away," Will said. "And you know she's not doing that alone. Costume duty. Ouch. That's why you need to find a *Mrs.* Davidson one of these days."

"Yeah, any day now," Joe said, then lowered his voice to a whisper. "Hey, did Darvell say what he wants to be this year?"

Will leaned in closer. "Some kind of robot called Voltron. How about Jimmy?"

"A fucking dragon," Joe whispered out of range of Lydia. "Can you believe that? Kid's already reading *The Hobbit*, and does he want to be an elf or a goblin? *Noooo*. He goes right for the dragon."

"Oh, man," Will said, laughing. "I'm sorry."

"Don't laugh," Joe said. "You and Cheryl gave him that book for his birthday."

"Hey, Darvell likes it too," Will said. "Can we help it if our kids are twice as smart as blue-collar stiffs like you and me? Besides, look on the bright side, man. At least he didn't ask to be the faery princess."

"I wish he did," Joe said. "No scales, no tail. No finding a way to have him breathe fire in public."

"You're right," Will said, louder now. "Did you hear Spitznagel's got them reading *Huck Finn*? Parts of it, at least. I mean, were we reading *Huckleberry Finn* in the fourth grade?"

"I couldn't spell Huckleberry in the fourth grade, much less read it."

"I can spell 'Huzzlebury,'" Lydia said. "A-B-C-D-E-F-G... "

"That's excellent, honey." Joe turned back to Will. "See what you started?"

"Yeah, I'd better go. Those two knuckleheads are probably turning my cruiser into the Starship Enterprise right about now." The two men shook hands as Will turned to go. "You got any plans for tonight? Hot date, I hope?"

"Oh, yeah. Me, the Queen, and the boob tube, I'm thinking."

Lydia stood up and clapped her hands. "We're having pizza with Sam and Rocky."

"Sam and Rocky?" Will said, rubbing his chin. "Sounds like a couple of old-time gangsters to me."

Joe scrambled. "Not really. Couple of guys I knew in Vietnam might be passing through town, is all."

"Well, have fun," Will said, grinning; it was clear he wasn't buying that one wholesale. "Okay if I drop Jimmy back about the same time tomorrow, on my way to work?"

"Sounds good." Joe waved as Will disappeared around the side of the house.

"I want to be a faery princess for Halloween," Lydia said. "Or the lady at the flower store."

"Queen, you can be anything you want," he said. "Just no dragons."

Without warning, she abandoned her notebook and rambled out to the lonely sycamore to hunt for caterpillars, although from her mouth the word came out more like "*cat pillows*." He liked the fact that she was creating an entirely new language, piece by piece. For Joe, bringing up a girl alone was the hardest part of being a dad. With the boy, his own father's simple approach had seemed to work—show up, and cheer like hell—but he felt completely lost when it came to Lydia. And she was only four; what happened when she was fourteen? He had enough problems letting her go out to the tree in the backyard alone. He didn't even want to think about the day he'd let her go out on a date. He hoped dating would be obsolete by the 1990s, just like board games and the eight-track tape.

He sat back down on the porch with a sigh, keeping an eye on his girl.

In his dream last night, he was riding in the backseat of a station wagon with Roxy. The car felt familiar; after a while he realized it was the same Nash Ambassador he'd grown up in back in Fargo. As far as he could tell, there was no one driving. Outside the windows, the sky was almost black and the car was careening back and forth on some invisible road, if there was a road at all. Roxy was balled up in the corner, crying, saying something he couldn't quite hear. Someone was chasing them. There was a set of white headlights piercing the darkness behind them, following their every move. Joe tried opening the door to try to jump, but it wouldn't budge. The car skidded and bucked like a roller coaster. He reached over the front seat for the steering wheel, but it was just out of reach. There was the rotten smell of sulfur in the air. As he looked out the windshield, he could see the faint outline of a highway in front of them. Suddenly the road ended at the edge of a cliff. Joe wrestled frantically with the handle on Roxy's door as they began to fall.

Roxy cradled the phone receiver to her ear, taking turns between putting on makeup and taking drags from the cigarette she had balanced on the edge of the sink. The bathroom was so cramped it might as well have been a phone booth. She kept the door open, listening for Sam sleeping in the living room. She wouldn't tell Betsy this, but she was listening for Joe, too.

Lately, talking to Betsy on the telephone had been an exercise in patience. All her cousin wanted to talk about these days was her boy, little Jan—or Miracle Jan, if she believed what Betsy told her about the kid's superhuman powers. There was nothing wrong with talking up your own child, Roxy knew that, but lately Betsy seemed to forget who was the one on the run.

They'd been on the line for almost a half hour now, and the whole time Betsy had been going on about—well, Roxy wasn't exactly sure. Maybe she wasn't listening very well. Joe would be there any minute, and these were definitely two worlds she didn't want colliding. Not yet, anyway.

"Betsy, sorry to interrupt—but you got any news for me?"

"Do I ever," Betsy said. "Did I tell you what happened at the county fair?"

Roxy rubbed the bridge of her nose. "Yeah, you did. An elephant escaped."

"Can you believe it? I mean, right here in Galilee County. They ain't caught it yet, neither. For all I know that elephant could be right outside my door right now. What would we do? We live so far from town, and Zeke don't keep no guns, of course, being a man of God and all. But I ask you, what would we do? We'd be in a real heap of trouble, I tell you that."

"Maybe Miracle Jan can talk to him in elephant," Roxy said under her breath. "I meant, do you have any news that concerns *me*? Maybe news about the Old Bear?"

She listened as Betsy yelled something to Jan about stealing Oreos from the box; apparently the miracle boy was now using his superpowers for petty theft. Then she heard her cousin pick the phone back up. "Afraid not, Roxy. Haven't heard much of anything. We're all alone out here at the house, you know. With Zeke back out on the kerosene circuit, it's just me and little Jan. Only soul ever comes to visit regular is your mom, and that's once in a blue moon."

Roxy took a drag from the cigarette, waving the smoke from the mirror. "Sheriff ain't been out to your place asking questions, has he?"

"If Rodriguez came out here, don't you think that'd be the first thing out my mouth?"

Roxy felt the urge to say *no*.

She was poking her head out into the living room every so often to check on Sam. Her roommate Desiree had gone ahead and duct-taped pillows to the sharp edges of the few pieces of furniture they did have. It wasn't exactly good for company, but the only company anyone got at the Happy Pharaoh Trailer Park was either carrying the good book or a badge. Or maybe just an eviction notice. Ever since Sam had started walking, everything had turned into a target for his forehead. He'd pick a target in the room, and *bam!* he was running at it like a midway daredevil. So far the kid had been more or less indestructible. Pretty soon they'd try shooting him out of a cannon.

"You need to bite the bullet and call Annie," Betsy said. "Send her a letter, at least. That woman sure misses you."

"It's complicated," Roxy said, not wanting to get into it. There were plenty of reasons why she hadn't called Annie or Louise, and most of them included having no clue what to tell them. Besides, the last thing she wanted was to get Annie in the middle of some kind of trouble; maybe it *was* paranoia, but she'd never forgotten what those Iowa truckers had said about cops being able to find you. And in the movies it was so easy to tap phones or follow a postmark. "If Rodriguez ever does show up and asks you questions, don't say anything, okay?"

"What would I say? Eight months, and you haven't told me much of anything. It's like we got a secret agent in the family. All I know for sure is you got a telephone and you're breathing. You haven't even told me if you've got a new man in your life."

"Why would I do that?" Roxy said, twisting the cord around her arm like a rattlesnake. "Listen, the last thing I'd want right now is a man." Outside she heard the low rumble of a truck engine that could have been Joe. "Look, I've got to go. I love you. I'll call you again in a few weeks."

"Love you and Sam too," Betsy said. "And be careful, girl." She hung up.

Roxy looked at herself in the mirror. Yeah, the last thing she wanted was a man. But here she was on Saturday night, checking herself in the mirror like a girl getting ready for prom. She finished her smoke and flushed it. She sure didn't feel like a girl at prom. She drew closer to the tiny mirror, her nose about touching the glass; she sure as hell didn't look like one, either. Every time she looked, there were new lines drawn on her face, connecting the dots with her freckles; this whole fugitive thing had not been easy on her complexion. Thirty-one was not the best time for a woman to go on the run.

For better or worse, it might have been the first time she felt exactly like her age.

The plan had always been simple: find someplace to hide out until things smoothed over back home with the law. Cairo had turned out to be as good a place as any to disappear: another crumbled Midwest town with a faint pulse, its slow-beating heart hidden beneath layers of abandoned storefronts and vacant lots. She'd picked up work right away waiting tables at a greasy spoon outside town called the Lunch Box, and she was sharing the double-wide with one of the other waitresses, Desiree, who had a five year-old-girl of her own. They offset shifts to look after each other's kid. There were plenty of motels in Cairo, but Roxy was done with motels. She was still looking over her shoulder—every time a cop sat at her station she reminded herself to breathe—but at least the days had stayed simple through the summer months as she waited for news from North Dakota.

Now things were getting complicated again.

A lot had changed since she'd abandoned the van in that parking lot back in January: she was blonde now, for one, thanks to Revlon. But more importantly, she hadn't had a drink in nine months; in a strange way, taking care of Sam made everything easier. It had taken all of spring and summer to really see herself as a mom. The world seemed clearer now; there were things that mattered, and things that didn't. She wasn't sure which category to put Joe Davidson in yet, but she knew she was falling for him, at the one moment in her life where she couldn't afford to fall for anything.

God knew it wasn't love at first sight. That snowy day back in January, Joe had dropped them off at the intersection of Routes 51 and 60 in Cairo—take a left and you cross over to Kentucky, take a right and you're in Missouri. They hadn't seen each other again until the one day in late May he'd come into the Lunch Box with a highway construction crew. He recognized her immediately, even with the time passed and the new hair; she must have made an impression. Their first date hadn't been a date. It had been a study in awkwardness, two single parents at the Calvert Drive-In trying desperately to remember what it was like to be sexy and cool.

She remembered every detail: it had been a hot day in July, and he'd picked her up in his work truck, officially the unsexiest vehicle in southern Illinois, with its fresh crust of sawdust and the hula girl on the dashboard still missing a head. Worse than that, he had chosen to take her to *Rocky III*. The lot was empty when they got there; he'd been off on the movie time by an hour. He also had parked them in the front row, so close they'd have to lean out the window to see more than anyone's torso on the screen. They sat in perfect silence for a while, his hands fastened tight to the wheel. "You want something from the snack bar?" He looked like he was about to jump from the truck and bolt for the woods any second. "I'm sorry. I'm a little out of practice with the whole dating thing."

She could remember wanting to bolt herself, but she *was* hungry. "Well, I don't know if this is a date or not," she had said. "But if it was, I'm pretty sure it's customary for the guy to bring the girl a double burger with cheese. With lots of waffle fries. And a Coke."

Well, Roxy thought, at least the complications came with a side of fries.

She was still in the bathroom, tying her long hair back from her face with a rubber band, when there was a rap at the screen door.

"Hey, Rock," Joe said, peering through the screen. "You two ready?"

Roxy came over and took the hook off the door. She pushed it open, but stood there for a moment blocking the doorway, kneading her hands together in tight circles. "Would it be all right if we wanted to get back here early—you know, later tonight?"

"Of course," he said. "You may want to come back even earlier when you see dinner." He hung his head like one of those soap opera doctors when surgery didn't go well. "Julia Child I am not." He pointed over to the truck parked about twenty feet away at the far end of the trailer. "My co-chef has fallen asleep in the backseat. Tough day at the office."

Roxy smiled. "Caterpillars?"

"Armies of caterpillars. A few of them might have made it into the mac and cheese, so be careful where you put your fork tonight."

"Hey, Queen," Roxy called out. She could only see the very top of her head in the back of the truck, but she waved anyway. "Well, there's always *pizza*," she said, loud enough for Lydia to hear; she knew the girl would eat pizza for breakfast if she could. "And I've got snacks for Sam in my bag, just in case." She opened the screen door wider for Joe; he held it with his boot while Roxy went into the kitchen. "My roommate's visiting her folks for the weekend," she said. "Come on in for a sec."

"Thanks," he said, standing halfway in the door. "But for some reason Queen gets mighty ornery whenever she wakes up alone." He saw the pillows taped to the chairs and coffee table. "He's still in his Evel Knievel phase, huh?" He looked over at Sam on the living room floor; he'd woken up now and was rolling around on a blanket, pushing around some kind of blue stuffed animal that wasn't easily identified. "*I pity the fool who don't like my mac and cheese,*" Joe growled, putting up his arms and throwing punches in the air. Sam instantly looked up and started to cackle.

Roxy turned from the cupboard to take a good, long look at this man: almost six-and-a-half feet tall with shoulders broad enough that he'd learned to walk sideways through most doors, and there he was, a complete clown in front of an eighteen-month-old boy. She would never tell him this, but it was the stupid little moments like this that made her want to say adios to the plan. After all, what was a plan worth if it didn't allow the good ones in?

"What's James up to tonight?" she said, getting some things together. "Let me guess: building a moon orbiter out of tin cans and Bondo."

"I wish," Joe said. "He's sleeping over at a friend's house. They'll probably play video games until the sun comes up. Sometimes I think that kid needs a little more danger in his life."

"Careful what you wish for."

He nodded, only half listening now; at the moment, his attention was locked into a staring contest with little Sam. The kid may only be a toddler, he thought, but he had the concentration of a chess master. Lydia used to do the same thing at that age, stare at something until it either smiled or disappeared. "Young Jimbo's got a school project due, too. You ready for this? The *diorama*."

"The dreaded diorama? Well, you wanted danger, my friend, and you got it."

"*Roman Empire*," Lydia announced all the way from the back seat of the truck, but from her mouth the words came out more like "*Women-and-Pie!*"

Joe and Roxy looked at one another, trying hard not to laugh. "Queen is up," Joe said.

"Well, I'm a woman, and I *love* pie," Roxy said. "Pecan especially."

"Say, Rocky," Joe bellowed, his face lit up like he was on stage. "Have you met Lydia?"

"Daddy, not *now*," the little girl pleaded. Even from a distance she knew what was coming, and she didn't like it. *"Please."*

"All right," he said, feigning disappointment. "All right."

The drive over to Joe's house was one of the few pleasures Roxy took from Cairo, Illinois. She got to see the old, wide streets on the other side of town, the kind city planners must have laid out with so much hope a hundred years ago when Cairo had been growing, its docks full of barges heading up and down the Mississippi and the Ohio. Joe's street reminded her of the one she had grown up on back in Nazareth, a long and straight dead end where the blacktop suddenly gave way to a horizon of rolling fields. It was the perfect dimensions for touch football, broad and slightly curved at the top with thick curbs. The house was just about perfect, too: three stories with a wraparound front porch and a back yard that must have been made for barbecues. The lone sycamore in the back looked straight out of a storybook, although if she had any say there would be a tire swing hanging from the lowest branch.

Joe pulled the truck to the curb in front of the house and cut the engine. "We've got a deck around back. We could watch the sun go down before dinner."

"I've been here before, Joe," she said, her hand finding his. "Remember?" She hadn't noticed before, but sitting this close to him, she noticed there was a fresh snowfall of sawdust in his beard. "Are we having wood chip stew or something?" she said, scratching a few of the tiny flakes with her fingers.

"It's a surprise," he said, trying his best to look mysterious. She liked the fact that for him, it was more or less impossible.

Two years ago the house had been a complete dump; Joe had the Polaroids to prove it. Missing gutters, holes in the floors, squirrels in the attic, snakes in the cellar, pegged hardwood floors warped by water damage. Joe had been working on a staircase in the house next door when the landlord let him move in rent-free in exchange for fixing the place up. People always asked him why he didn't just buy the place outright, but for Joe, Cairo had always been temporary.

Roxy liked it when he talked about his work: here was a man who got excited talking about gables and soffits. He was a builder, and that was the exact opposite of every other man she'd known.

Lydia insisted on unlocking the front door herself, so Joe put the key in her hands and guided them toward the lock. It took about five minutes. Once the door was open, Lydia scampered straight up to her room, climbing the tall staircase with her hands as much as her feet.

Joe turned to Roxy and cleared his throat. "Now close your eyes," he said as they stood on the porch. "You too, Sam."

The boy wobbled, looking up at Joe with a dazed expression.

"Close enough," Joe said. He guided Roxy through the front door and into the foyer, his big hands covering her eyes. She could feel the calluses on his palms; she liked the roughness of his skin against her cheeks. "Okay," he said. "Open."

When she opened her eyes, there was a crib with a giant red bow on it standing at the foot of the stairs. She put her hand over her mouth.

"It's teakwood," he said. "I salvaged it from a deck I replaced a few weeks ago. I know Sam will probably be ready for a bed soon, so I made the sides come off pretty easy." He stood next to it, beaming. "So, you like it?"

She ran her palm slowly along the smooth rim of sandy grey wood as if she was touching a piece of art in a museum. It was truly beautiful. "Joe, I don't know if I can accept this," she said. "I can't pay you back."

"Since when do you have to pay me back?" he said. "Look, I'm a carpenter. Your kid needed a crib, so I made him a crib. If I was a baker, he'd get apple turnovers or something, right?"

Roxy didn't answer. She didn't say anything for a while, just kept running her hand over the smooth wood. "You made this."

Sam had already stumbled over and knocked into the corner of the crib with his head. Luckily, every part of it was rounded and smooth. He looked up at Roxy and mimicked her, putting his hands on the bars, too.

Joe stood still, trying to get a read from Roxy's face. "Well, try it out. See if he likes it."

She hoisted Sam into the middle of the crib; he sat there with the same dazed look on his face. At eighteen months, he had about ten words in his repertoire—words in English anyway—but he wasn't saying anything. The boy leaned down and grabbed at the blanket with both hands; it had little spaceships and planets on it.

"That was Jimmy's choice," Joe said. "I would have gone for cowboys myself."

She was getting that queasy feeling in the pit of her stomach, the one that suddenly came on when things started to get complicated. "I don't know if this will fit through the door of our trailer, Joe."

"Well," he said, twisting the toe of his boot into the floor. "I was hoping you'd want to leave it here."

It took three readings of *Billy Goats Gruff* for Lydia to finally drift off to sleep. When Joe came back from Lydia's room, Roxy was sitting on the edge of his bed, still dressed, slowly getting used to the size of the place; after Joe had knocked down a wall, the master bedroom was about the same square footage as her share of the trailer. Joe moved around the bed and sat down on the other side; for a while they just listened to each other breathe. It kind of reminded him of the drive-in, when they had both wanted to make a break for it. It would be harder now, though, since there were sleeping children involved.

Besides, the sex was fantastic.

"I've never been in a house with a *back* staircase before," she said, unlacing her shoes and kicking them to the floor. "They made two, just in case one was out of order?"

"Servant's stairs," he said. "They weren't kidding when they built this place. If you're good, I'll take you up and show you the observatory."

"And if I'm bad?"

"Then you get the dungeon tour. I think they still have a few stiffs chained to the wall down there, so be careful." He looked over at the battered clock radio on the nightstand, with its numbers that turned over like the departure board at a train station. He wondered if this was a good time to tell Roxy about his dream; he wondered if there was a good time at all. He wanted to know everything about her, but he didn't want to push her away, either. He wanted to ask her what she was running from, but he didn't know how. "How sad is this? Eight-thirty on a Saturday and I'm already getting in bed."

"Yeah, but you're getting into bed with me," she said. "Big difference."

He unlaced his boots and slipped them off. As he sat there and slid out of his jeans, he could feel her fingers drawing pictures on the small of his back.

Downstairs, there was a knock on the front door. Joe swiveled around, and they looked at each other for a moment. He sprang up and went to the window; he couldn't see the porch from the bedroom, but there was a police cruiser parked across the street, right behind his truck.

"Who is it, Joe?" There was a slight pitch of panic behind her voice.

"Cairo's finest," he said, trying to come off nonchalant. "I'll go down, see what they want." He slipped his jeans back on, lumbered down the steps in his bare feet and opened the door. Will Barnett stood on the porch with another deputy, a skinny kid with a buzz cut he'd never met before.

"Hey, Will," Joe said, ruffling his shaggy hair. "What's up?"

Will looked at him with an embarrassed smile. "Guess who left his video games at home," he said. "Cheryl called here a few hours ago but I guess you were out. Anyway, we were in the neighborhood, so I thought I'd go ahead and pick them up. Sorry if it's too late."

"You kidding? It's not even nine. Wait here a second, I know where they are." He didn't want to let them in, only for fear of making Roxy more scared than she probably already was.

Sure enough, when he got to the living room the little black cartridges were still stacked on top of the television. He scooped them up and padded back to the front door.

"Thanks," Will said. "This is my new partner, by the way, Lee Connolly. Lee, this is the man who fixed the roof at the station, so you owe him a lot."

"My desk thanks you," Lee said. "No more wet paperwork."

They shook hands. Lee looked about twenty-two, and he still had a boy's face, red and plumped with baby fat. Joe noticed the familiar neon pink of Sheriff's Raffle tickets sticking out of his shirt pocket; Cairo was a poor town in an even poorer county, and even the police had to find ways to pay the mortgage and the utility bills.

Joe pointed to the tickets. "What's the big prize this year?"

"First prize is a washer/dryer. Second prize is a trip to Mexico," Lee said.

"Mexico? Well that sold me," Joe said. "You can put me down for a half dozen."

They talked for a few minutes more, mostly about the Cubs losing Andre Dawson again and the Bears' season opener coming up. Joe saw them to the end of the porch, then waved good-bye as they got back into their car and made a slow U-turn, disappearing down the street and around the corner.

When Joe got back upstairs, the bed was empty, the room dark. "Rocky?"

He went into Sam's room, thinking she was checking on the boy, but the crib was empty, too. Suddenly, his skin turned hot. He ran into the bathroom, then downstairs to the living room; he opened doors to rooms he'd barely seen before, even in daylight. When he got to the kitchen he saw the back door was open, cool night air filtering in.

"Hey, Rock?" he called out, the backyard dark. It was a clear night, but the moon was only a sliver on the horizon. He stepped out onto the back porch and stood silent, trying to listen. In the distance he thought he heard a child's cry. Maybe it was one of those feral cats that prowled the field for mice, yowling in heat. Joe stepped off the back stoop, his bare feet rustling through the wet grass. "Rocky, you out here?" He felt his way back toward the sycamore.

It was too dark to see, but he could hear her raspy breathing from inside the hollow of the tree. "Rocky, it's me, it's Joe. Everything's all right. They were just selling raffle tickets."

After a few moments, he felt a hand grab onto his forearm and squeeze tight. Roxy's palm was sweaty and shaking. He put his hand on top of hers, then ran it up her arm until he found her face. Her cheeks were wet with tears. They stayed like that for a while, not saying anything, the boy coughing now and then but staying quiet as the three of them huddled together.

"I got scared," she said with a tone of embarrassment.

"I don't blame you," he said. "They wanted ten bucks a ticket."

Roxy managed a shaky laugh, holding onto him even tighter.

When they got back to the house, there was crying coming from upstairs—Lydia had awoken to a completely empty house. Joe groaned; this was going to be a night for putting out fires. He hurtled the back steps up to her room.

Roxy followed behind with Sam, taking him to his room to settle the sleepy boy back into his crib. "You're still better at this than I am," she whispered. "You're a little outlaw, all right."

When Sam looked like he was on his way back to a dream, Roxy padded down the hall and stood quietly outside Lydia's room. She peeked through the crack in the door to see Joe sitting at the foot of the bed, his little girl sitting straight up at the other end with her arms folded, her face screwed into a little scowl.

Roxy took a chance and opened the door. "How's it going in here?"

"Hello, Rock," Joe said; there was that vaudeville face again. "Say, have you met Lydia?"

Roxy rolled her eyes as she stepped in the room. "Lydia? No, I don't think I have," she said, already knowing what came next. It seemed to be working; the girl's face was already melting into an uneasy smile.

Joe leapt over and scooped the girl off the bed. *"Lydia, oh Lydia, say have you met Lydia? Lydia the Tattooed Lady. She has eyes that folks adore so, and a torso even more so,"* he sang, his big paws clasped around her tiny waist as he twisted her in the air above the bed. She was dizzy with delight, laughing out loud and trying to catch her breath at the same time. *"Oh Lydia, the Queen of Tattoo! On her back is the Battle of Waterloo! Beside it the Wreck of the Hesperus too—you can learn a lot from Lydia!"*

They twirled like that for a while, a father and daughter dancing weightless in the air.

The sudden rush of energy spent, Lydia was sleepy again. Roxy backed out of the room and closed the door as Joe tucked

Lydia back under the covers and kissed her forehead. "Good night, Queen of Tattoo," he whispered as he turned out the light.

In the hallway, Roxy waited for Joe to close the door before she kissed him.

He put his arms around her. "You know, we named her Lydia just so I could sing that song," he said, out of breath. "I should probably learn another verse one of these days."

"I hope she doesn't mind me staying over," Roxy said, resting her head on his chest as they stood together. Even without his shoes, he was at least a foot taller. Roxy felt safe here. "Does she remember her mom at all?"

He shook his head. "She was too young. But we've got plenty of pictures. It's James that might see things as a little— complicated. Nine-year-old boys can get pretty territorial."

"Hence the convenient sleepover at Darvell's house," she said. "Nice work, Machiavelli."

They kissed again.

Joe kept his arms around her waist and they danced together in a slow circle. "So are you going to tell me who Machiavelli is?"

"Come on," she said, taking his hand and leading him back to the bedroom. "I've got so much I want to tell you."

The weekend before Halloween, Joe backed his truck into the Happy Pharaoh Trailer Park and moved all of Roxy and Sam's stuff over to the house. It only took one trip. There was an excuse: Desiree was moving back to Galesburg to live with her folks, and Roxy couldn't afford the rent by herself. But they really didn't need an excuse. Maybe Lydia was the happiest about it, since she could now think up a new outfit for Sam to try on whenever she wanted. James treated the new living arrangements as more of a pest invasion, however; he took care to stay away from parts of the house that might be infested.

It was Monday when Roxy was sitting on the front porch enjoying the midday sun and a rare day off. She had the scattered makings of a dragon tail stretched out across her lap. Maybe this would melt the lump of coal in the boy's heart, she thought; she'd spent all morning cutting silver fabric into scales. She wanted to surprise him with the peace offering. While she sat there working, she practiced the conversation she was bound to have with the neighbors when they wondered why there was a strange woman hanging out at Joe Davidson's house.

"Howdy! I'm Joe's long-lost sister, Sheila. Damn pleased to meet ya!"

"Bonjour! I am zee new au pair, Monique!"

There was the truth, of course, but she was only just getting used to the truth in explaining things to Joe, much less strangers. She'd told him just about everything by now—about Sam, about Dill, about that night at the Motel de Love—and he still wanted her to move in with him. Obviously, the man was crazy. Or maybe a late-blooming psycho-killer, after all.

She had just come back out from checking on Sam in his crib when she noticed James jogging up the street, alone. Her wristwatch said noon; last time she checked, school let out at two-thirty. She knew his class had a field trip that day to a local dairy farm, but that was probably miles away. The kid didn't even have his bookbag on him.

"Hey, stranger," she called as he came closer. "You lost?"

He stopped at the foot of the porch steps but didn't look her in the eye. "My dad here?"

"You know he's fixing the roof at your school this week." She put out her hand, reaching for his shoulder. "You okay, kiddo? What are you doing home so early?"

"I don't have to tell you anything," he said, recoiling. "You're not my mom."

"No, I'm not," she said, shoving the folds of fabric aside. "I'm just the dumb broad making a dragon costume because she's got nothing better to do."

The boy folded his arms, looking like he was about to run all the way back to wherever it was he'd just come from. From all the sweat drenching his pants and shirt, she guessed somewhere in South America.

Roxy leaned back on her arms and sighed; she could remember having this same conversation twenty-five years ago, only she had been the sore kid at the bottom of the steps and Annie was the one sitting on the porch covered with dragon scales. Or something like that.

"Listen, James, I know how you feel: you think you have to be the guardian angel of remembering your mom. When I was your age, my dad left home, and he never came back. You miss your mom, and you want to make sure everyone else misses her. I get it. But take how much you miss her, and then triple it. That's how much your dad misses her," she said. "He's always going to miss her. Nothing's ever going to change that."

"Do you love my dad?" It was more of an accusation than a question.

The kid had caught her off guard. She swallowed hard. "My life would probably be a lot easier if I didn't," she said.

"So you love him."

"Yes," she said. "If you smiled a little more, I might love you, too."

James stood there for a while, rocking back and forth on the balls of his feet. Then he sat down on the top step, glad to be off his feet. Resentment or not, he seemed like a boy in desperate need of an ally. "We had a field trip today in school. Mrs. Spitznagel took us to a farm."

"I heard about that. Sounds wonderful."

"Yeah, well," he said, kneading his hands. "Me and Darvell kind of started up a tractor. And we kind of drove it into a fence."

"You're kidding," she said. "Was anyone hurt?"

"No, it was only like three miles an hour," he said. "But we knocked down a fence, and all the cows got out all over the place. Old Spitzy got pretty mad."

"I bet. So you both ran home?"

Now he looked her in the eye. "You would too if you saw Mrs. Spitznagel."

"Good point."

As they talked some more, they could both hear the rumble of Joe's truck coming down the street.

James shot up so fast his glasses almost flew off his nose. "He's gonna be pissed," he said, the color draining from his face. "He's gonna kill me."

Roxy bit her lip to hide a smile; for all his size, she couldn't imagine Joe Davidson hitting anyone in anger, much less his own son. "I've got an idea," she said. "Why don't you head up to your room, and I'll wait here and feel him out—you know, check him for weapons."

"Good idea," the boy said, already halfway to the door. "Thanks."

Joe looked like he had a good head of steam when he got out of the truck; someone at the school must have already told him about the Great Cow Break of 1983. He blew past Roxy on the porch but stopped at the door, like there was some kind of invisible spell preventing him from going inside. He turned back, taking a few deep breaths to calm down. He still had roofing guards strapped on his legs.

"He's upstairs," she said. "He thinks you're going to get rough with him."

This was new to her, being the voice of reason. And for a second, Roxy thought she'd actually be a little scared right now if she didn't know him the way she did. Finally, he came back and slumped down on the steps next to her.

"I spanked him when he was six years old," he said. "I hated it more than he did. Never wanted to do it again."

She put an arm around him, drawing him closer. "Listen, it's none of my business, but I saw the look on that boy's face when you were driving up here just now. Trust me, I don't think he needs any punishment worse than what he's already got."

"Well, there's one thing that boy needs," he said. "Driving lessons. Did you know they ran straight through a cow pen? There was a cow in the drive-through lane at the Dairy Barn. They even found a couple wading in the Ohio. There's cows all over Cairo."

"Honey, there's always cows all over Cairo."

He picked up one of the dragon scales and rubbed the fabric between his fingers. "He looked really scared, huh?" he said, a smile escaping his lips. "Like, how scared?"

"Scale of one to ten, I'd say fourteen," she said, making a sour face. "Not half as scared as the other kids are going to be when they see this dragon, though. I found a way to get the nostrils to puff smoke. Hello, baby powder."

He picked up the dragon head. "Wow. Rock, you don't have to do this."

"You know, you are so right," she said. "That's probably why I'm doing it."

The Lunch Box was decked out in orange and black streamers for Halloween. There was a scarecrow roped to a pole out on the road that was supposed to be the Headless Horseman but there was no horse, so he hung there alone to frighten the crows that loitered on each side of the highway. They made the waitresses dress up—Roxy was a sexy witch—and the daily special on the chalkboard was pumpkin pancakes. She picked up the two dollars someone had left her on the counter; she'd never get rich on the tips here, that was for sure. The Lunch Box was the kind of place where teenagers wanted a cheeseburger at six in the morning and old folks came in wanting breakfast at four in the afternoon.

Roxy took a rag out of her apron and wiped down the counter, glad for the break in the midday rush. She looked at the clock; she'd gotten used to Joe coming in most days right around this time and sitting at her station. Hell, she thought, *I've gotten used to a lot of things the last couple months.* There would always be that part of her that wondered how long it would last. No matter how long she stayed in one place, she'd always be on the run. It wasn't fair, but that's the way it was. She felt bad for Joe. She felt bad about not calling Betsy in almost a month, too.

She was waiting on a couple of orders when she looked up and stared out the front window into the parking lot. There was Joe, coming toward her from his truck, walking and talking with another man.

Her heart lurched; the other guy was a *cop.*

She was just off her break, so she couldn't duck out back. What the hell was Joe thinking?

As they came in the diner both men were both laughing hard, slapping each other's back like a couple of teenagers after the big game. Or maybe a couple of sailors after liberty call.

"Rocky, this is my friend Will," Joe said, sliding into the empty stool in front of her. He sure seemed happy enough. "He's a sheriff's deputy."

"I can see that," she said, trying to act busy in front of them; she hadn't taken her eyes off the badge on this guy's jacket since they had come in. The back of her neck started to get a little sweaty. "Your son is Darvell, right?"

"Afraid so," he said. "So you're Rocky. Good to finally meet you. Funny, you sure don't look like a gangster. Or a Vietnam vet, either."

She turned to Joe, looking for some kind of an explanation, but he was avoiding the heat of her stare, pretending to look over a menu, even though he'd been in that place so often he probably had the thing memorized. Roxy rested a fist on her hip. "What's going on here, Joe?"

Will eased onto the next stool. "Can I get two coffees to go? Got my partner out in the car; I can only stay a minute."

She swiveled around and lifted a couple of to-go cups from the stack to pour out two coffees from the urn. She still wasn't sure what was going on, but for some reason she had a good feeling. She trusted Joe; she remembered him talking about his friend Will Barnett a few times; he must have forgotten to mention his best friend in Cairo happened to be a deputy sheriff.

"Thank you, Rock," Will said, reaching for the sugar. "You know, Joe asked me to do some snooping for a friend of his," he said, pouring sugar into his cup. "So I did a little snooping."

A nervous smile escaped her lips. "Joe has friends?"

"Yeah, and a *lady* friend even." Will reached around to his back pocket and pulled out a crumpled notepad. "Long story short: the news from North Dakota is all good. No warrants on this mysterious lady friend," he said, flipping through a few pages. "Not even a parking ticket. But they got a real potboiler going on up there in Galilee County, let me tell you. Seems the sheriff just up and died a couple weeks ago."

Roxy's jaw dropped. "Severo Rodriguez is *dead*?" she said. "You're sure?" She was so loud even the old couple in the back booth stopped eating for a moment, poking up their heads, on the lookout for trouble.

Will looked at the pad again, trying to read his own writing. "Sev-uh-ro Rodriguez, yes ma'am, that's correct. You must know this anonymous friend of Joe's. The story gets better, though; seems this Rodriguez fella was crooked as a frozen snake. Soon as he died, someone made an anonymous call to the state cops, and now they're all over that place. Feds, too: they're talking about payoffs, phony contracts, illegal stills. Maybe even murder." He shook his head as he read his pad, whistling like he was turning the pages on a dime-store thriller. "Anyway, regarding one Roxy Rebecca Boone, I can tell you no one's looking at her for anything. They did have a warrant out for her husband—guy by the name of Dill Pembo—but he's back inside since July, on a parole violation. So, coast is clear—well, except for one thing."

The smile on Roxy's face suddenly disappeared. "What's that?"

Will blew on his coffee and took a slow sip. "She still owes three dollars and twenty cents in late fees to the Nazareth Public Library." He shrugged his shoulders. "Hey, when I snoop, I go all out."

A conspiratorial smile spread across Joe's face. "We owe you, man."

"Yeah," Roxy said, still dazed. Suddenly she felt about a hundred pounds lighter. "How can we pay you back?"

"Ma'am, you can send me a postcard," Will said with a smile. "Never been to North Dakota myself. Joe tells me it's a whole other world up there." He lifted himself up from the stool and picked up his hat from the counter. "Sounds like you two might have a lot to talk about, so I'll go ahead and see myself out."

That night, Joe Davidson had another dream. They were in the station wagon again. But this time they were in the front seat looking out at a clear blue sky. Roxy was searching for something on the radio with one hand and she had the other out the window, riding the warm breeze. The kids were in the back, restless as three wolverines. The road was straight and wide, and although he couldn't quite place the scenery, it felt a lot like North Dakota. After a while they stopped in front of a house, out in the middle of the rolling prairie. It had a big old mailbox out front and a tire swing around back. He had never seen the house before, but it felt like home.

Song of Simeon

Spring 1984

I am older than North Dakota. I am older than any farmhouse or fence post or deep well dug for cattle or sugar beets. I am older than the roads. Only the rocks and the Lakota belong to this place longer than me. I am not sure how old I am in years and months, but last summer people from Bismarck come to tell me I am the oldest man in the world. I am on the television. They tell me there is a woman in Japan older than me. One day the people from Bismarck put me on the telephone with the woman in Japan. It is her birthday. She does not speak English but I remember enough of her language to say hello I am calling to wish you a happy birthday.

She says *arrigato*. She says what took you so long?

I am a man ready to die. Why must this be sad? I am happy. I do not say I am waiting to die I say I am ready. All life is waiting. When you are ten you wait for twenty and when you are twenty you wait for forty but when you are my age if you wait for something that has not yet come you are in trouble. Today I am no longer waiting. The good book says Methuselah lived to be 969 years old. I imagine children from the local school writing him letters with dumb questions, too, always in October when teachers decide it is time to practice letter-writing skills. What is your secret Old Methuselah? Do you remember your first kiss? Do you like bananas? Did your father Enoch ever catch you in a lie?

I get a lot of dumb questions. The young men in Nazareth look at the parched arroyos of my face as if they were carved before the Flood. Do you drink Ole Simonson? Do you still feel desire?

What's your secret Ole Simonson?

I drink

I feel desire

And I have many secrets

My dreams are still clear. My memory slowly fades like withered branches cut away to keep the tree alive but when I sleep the people I once knew are sharp and clear in my mind. My dreams are silent pictures they do not depend on language. When I sleep my friends speak to me in silent voices like we are underwater. But when I am awake I am alone. I wake up at dawn after dreaming and sit around my empty house. The only regular visit I get is the Meals on Wheels lady on Tuesdays. The girl Annie tries to stop by but I know she is busy. Once I give her husband Joachim a loan to build the auto shop so she feels she owes me something even though he is long gone. We drink coffee and she asks me to tell stories about the old days but I am afraid because stories depend on words and even a young child knows words come and go as they please. When I am awake I am frightened because memory moves quickly like weather or ghosts it passes through my eyes in spotted sepia like old photographs left to broil and bubble in sunlight

but oh I dream in bright colors
　　when I sleep the world looks like the Wizard of Oz
　　　　the door opens
Glinda's lips move like hot streaks of burgundy
　　　　　　　white fields of poppies
　　　　sleep

When I no longer see the ghost dance in my dreams I know
I am ready. For a hundred years I have had the same dream.
I know this is hard to understand. They come in the night,
wearing the ghost shirts tasseled with eagle feathers and
claws and painted with moon sun and stars black crescent
moon painted on each cheek dancing around the giant pine
moaning wailing shrieking taking up handfuls of dust to wash
their hands throwing it over their heads until all I can see is
dust
　　　hard alkali soil crushed into fine white powder
　　　　　　　like they are dancing on the moon
　　I still see the woman falling
　　　　　her husband breaking into the chain to cover her
　　I was there
　　I still see Kicking Bear crying with his visions of God
　　　　　　　　　　　Father I come

I have never married. As far as I know I have no children.
Maybe I do not feel I deserve that happiness. When people ask
I make up stories about a wife long ago since there is no one
here old enough to prove me wrong. Both my imaginary sons
died in old wars. Lucius my youngest boy crossed into Canada
to enlist under a false name and was lost at Belleau Wood. I still
have a letter he wrote.

I wish I could say I have done good things for this lonely corner of the world but as I near death I can only recall the bad. Right now I am thinking of Severo Rodriguez. I am ashamed to say this but in a way he comes to Galilee County because of me. I meet him long before anyone calls him Old Bear. People call those times the dirty thirties. I am working for ACLU lawyers in the Red River Valley, translating for the *braceros* working the bonanza farms between Fargo and Grand Forks. They tell the lawyers their stories. The *braceros* are the hardest working people I have ever seen with eighteen hour days pulling sugar beets and dirt for pay. You have to walk a mile to wash your face in clean water. A company from Hollywood is here too making cowboy pictures. They make two a week with the same actors dressed in different clothes. One day you are the hero the next you are the villain. Much later I learn one of them is named John Wayne. On Sundays the motion picture company comes to the camps to ask the *braceros* if they will dress up like indians.

I am sitting inside a white tent with the lawyers and a *bracero* who will not give his name in Spanish or in English. He is probably no older than sixty but his face is like a chewed piece of bubble gum. His son waits for him outside the tent smoking a cigarette. I lean on the table and try speaking to the man in Huasteca even though I know only a few words. When I speak he looks up at me with sharp eyes as if I have insulted him. I am not from Mexico he says in English. I am American like you. He mumbles something in Spanish I cannot hear then folds his arms on the table and closes again like a clam.

Outside in the hot sun the son offers me a cigarette. We sit and smoke in the shade and watch the river drift past. Both banks have been dug up with countless tent poles and makeshift roads. A few wildcat oil rigs sunk in the dirt like crooked teeth. Across from us a gang is trying to free a steam thresher that has slipped into fresh mud with planks and a couple mules. Men from the American Crystal Sugar Company watch the lawyers' tent from a parked car.

You know my father will not talk to them.

I know. He doesn't like lawyers?

The young man shrugs. He doesn't like anybody. You should see how he treats the priest. To him, they are all crazy. *Curandero loco.* For him there is only work. Work and suffering.

He wipes his hand on his dusty shirt and holds it out. My name is Severo. And you?

I shake his hand. Ole Simonson.

He finishes his smoke and tosses it at the river. Is all North Dakota like this?

Head west and you'll see some of the most beautiful country in the world.

El tierra baldia? I hear that is rough country.

I guess it is a little rough. But it is beautiful.

And you live there?

All my life. A little town called Nazareth, in Galilee County.

Good fishing?

Most lakes are alkali but the Little Missouri runs close by. Muskies bigger than your leg.

It is almost twenty years later when Severo Rodriguez runs for sheriff of Galilee County and wins. I remember it is the same year they dam up the Little Missouri to make Lake Sakakawea. He defeats Jack Weeding because there is a bank robbery in Nazareth a month before. A man is shot on the street in broad daylight. Severo comes in and closes down the farm stills and puts some of the blind-piggers in jail. He builds a park and a hospital. He smiles at children so people think he's doing a good job. I think so too until I start hearing about the bad things.

The dam floods about a quarter of the Fort Berthold reservation. Towns like Old Salish and Van Hook are put underwater, the Mandan and Hidatsa who live there move to a new town on the edge of the new lake. On maps the town is named New Town. The Mandan call it Vanish. I hear someone is planning to build a casino there. The Mandan believe there was once a great flood that covered the earth. Their people are saved by building a great ship. When the waters of the Great Deluge recede the ship comes to rest somewhere in the hills southeast of what is now Lake Sakakawea. For thousands of years the Mandan call these the Holy Hills. In the good book, when Methuselah sees the boat his grandson Noah is building, the old man knows he will not live to see the Deluge. I picture him looking to the sky and waiting for the rain, hoping to catch the first cold drops on his parched tongue

> nine hundred year-old feet ache to splash in fat puddles
> shoulders finally grow weary
> > > eyes close
> > > > dreaming of the first rainbow

In my dream of the ghost dance Kicking Bear always comes over to greet me. He knows my father. As a boy I chased toads with his son Rain in the Face. I am happy to see Kicking Bear again but when I wake up I am wet with sweat. I want to tell him I believe. For a hundred years after that day at Pine Ridge when I stood with the horse soldiers I wake up shouting

> I believe you I believe you I do
> > oh God let your servant depart in peace
> > > because I believe

My full name is Ole Lincoln Simonson and my sisters are Birget Grant and Unn Antietam Simonson. That is how I know we are born during the War. There were no birth certificates then. When our mother and father come to America their

English is not so good. Their sense of direction must be worse because they are headed for Mississippi to help run a jewelry store. Somehow they find themselves pushing west from St. Paul reaching what was then called Dakota Territory a few weeks before the first frost. The Hunkpapa summer there and keep their distance, bewildered: a man and his pregnant woman building a lodge alone on the edge of the badlands. Luckily my mother makes pies good enough to prevent wars.

I am a small boy when the buffalo hunters pass by in bands of ten or twenty on their way to find the summer herds. I do not see their faces only harsh sunlight behind them but I remember their smell like cooking oil and gunpowder.

Hallo, my father calls out to them. Are you having knowledge of the States War? The *Amerikanske borgerkrigen*? His English is still not very good. But he has no need for English here. He only needs Norsk to speak to his wife and children and Lakota to speak with his friends.

You mean the War Between the States? Been over for years, friend. Lee surrendered to Grant in Pennsylvania.

And of Honest Abraham Lincoln?

Lincoln's dead, friend. Shot him in the head.

The closest town is Pile of Bones in Canada. What they now call Regina. Round trip it takes my father ten days ride to bring back flour and sugar and wood and nails and books. Crates of books. My father does not read unless it is the good book but he brings back any books he sees in windows English French Spanish Latin Portuguese. Books on making dresses, books on the Amazon, books on Roman history it does not matter I read them all. I read *Ivanhoe* to Rain in the Face and we joust like Saxon knights on painted ponies. Birget and Unn do not want to be Rebecca or Rowena they want to ride ponies too and siege the castle my father knows as the mud barn

in the fall we watch the buffalo hunters pass again on their
way back east
   wagons and pack mules snaked in a long dog-tired train
      sagging with stacks of buffalo hides
 prairie wolves linger downwind
     following the stale metal tang of dried blood

It is still spring when the people from Bismarck come back to
tell me I am now the oldest person in the world. This means
the lady in Japan is now dead but they do not say this out loud.
I am told there is a sturgeon fish still lurking in Devils Lake that
is older than me but there are only stories. I hope I do not have
to call him on his birthday. They tell me it is almost 1985 and
soon we will see a new millennium do you think you will live to
see the new millennium?
    I know I will not be alive then
        I hope I can
        finish
          telling you why

I am a young man when I see the ghost dance. North Dakota is
only a year old. A crying baby. Even here on the prairie we hear
about the prophet Jack Wilson and his visions of God in the
deserts of what is now called New Mexico. Some say he is
a messiah. The indian agents are frightened when they see the
Lakota dance the ghost dance in great numbers and they call in
the army.
 Kicking Bear comes over to greet me his broad face painted
with black moons
        Hau kola! Hepela!

I grip his elbow and say hello back. Pilamaya ye, thunkashila matho. Hepela kola.

He sees I am with horse soldiers from Fort Berthold. Their lieutenant is a thin boy with bright Irish hair not much older than me who does not speak Lakota. Kicking Bear knows English he also knows Metis French and a little Norsk but I know he does not want to talk to the lieutenant. I am only here to translate but now I worry Kicking Bear and Short Bull will think I am with the soldiers.

Mr. Simonson, tell kicking bear the ghost dance is illegal.

Kicking Bear I say he wants you to know the ghost dance is against the law.

Ask the colonel what law he is talking about.

Kicking Bear calls all horse soldiers colonel.

I ask the lieutenant.

Why, the law of the United States. This is the state of North Dakota now. Year of our Lord 1890.

Kicking Bear grunts. Does he know the ghost dance comes from his God? Does he know the ghost dance asks for his messiah to come?

I do not think he knows this. The soldiers think it is a war dance.

> *Tell the colonel I have had a vision*
> *of a child born of a virgin mother.*
> *He will be born here in these hills and become a man.*

I say you do not want me to tell the colonel that.

Hokahe hokshila! You must. The ghost dance is a gift from your God. The army will not listen to the Lakota but they will listen to you.

The lieutenant has been staring off into the sky as we talk but now he stamps his foot in the ground impatiently. If they do not stop then by God we will stop them. He rubs the grip of his pistol with his gloved hand. This is meant to intimidate Kicking

Bear. The lieutenant is too young to know Kicking Bear fought at Greasy Grass. Those who came back say he was the one to shoot Colonel Custer in the heart and then again above the eye.

Tell the colonel of my vision. You must.

I cannot tell him that. He will get angry.

We are not afraid we are wearing the ghost shirt which bullets cannot pierce. Do you believe in my vision Ole Simonson?

I look away.

You do not believe in my vision of God?

I believe you have a vision. I do not believe a messiah will be born in these hills of a virgin mother and save the world. That's too much to believe.

Kicking Bear looks at me like he has lost one of his sons. He turns away. You will believe, Ole Simonson. You are a young man now, but before you die, you will believe.

About a hundred miles south at Wounded Knee Creek in South Dakota three hundred Minneconjou and Hunkpapa Lakota will die that winter wearing their ghost shirts, men women and children cut down by machine guns and put into mass graves. Kicking Bear's brother Big Foot. Rain in the Face and his new wife. The army will put Kicking Bear and Short Bull in prison for a year and then let them out to work for Buffalo Bill Cody's circus show. They will ride around the ring on painted ponies in Schenectady and St. Louis holding targets for Annie Oakley. Everyone will cheer as they ride by.

Until the day of the bank robbery I believe my dreams are only dreams. Kicking Bear's words haunt me as I grow old but I believe they are only words. The robbers come out of the bank but their car will not start. Men spill out of Hovelsrud's pool hall into the street. Women press their faces against the windows of the beauty parlor and the Nifty Shoppe. Someone runs to get Jack Weeding. The robbers try to make for the Soo Line tracks in the middle of town maybe get lucky and catch a freight to at least get out of town. But they are surrounded. One of the robbers grabs a young woman crossing the street in front of the Dakota theatre and holds a gun to her head. The crowd closes tighter. An old man who was standing in line at the bank tries to plead with them to let the girl go. I am this man. I get too close and one of them shoots me twice almost point blank in the chest. As I lie there in the middle of the street life spilling out of me I think it is better for me to go, an old man instead of a young girl. I am an old man ready to die. I mumble words praying the Lord take me swiftly.

I should be dead instantly but I do not die.

They drag me into the pool hall and lay me on a table and fetch the doctor. There is no hospital then. The next day the young doctor says I honestly do not know how you are alive Ole Simonson but you are. He is smiling but his eyes are afraid like there is something inside me he does not understand. He says praise the Lord.

Yes praise the Lord I say.

A miracle.

Yes a miracle.

The doctor is whispering now. Excuse me for saying this but you don't seem so surprised to be alive. I mean to say, if I was shot two times in the heart from about a foot away I wouldn't expect to wake up. Especially at your age. But here you are, sitting up in bed and talking to me like you got influenza.

Maybe the Lord is not done with me yet.

But you must be ninety if you're a day. Just how old are you anyway?

I look out the window.

He shakes his head. A miracle.

Praise the Lord I say.

The young doctor is retired now. He lives on his daughter's ranch over in Montana. His legs aren't so good anymore. All those house calls he says. We talk on the telephone now and then. I still call him the young doctor. When we talk there is always this hitch in his voice like he wants to ask me about that day. He seems to understand there are things I cannot say.

How do you feel? I say on the telephone.

Oh like hell. Can't even get to the john under my own power anymore. I guess when you get old the legs are the first to go.

What do you know? I say. You are only seventy-five. A boy.

Are you ever going to tell me what happened that day?

A miracle.

Fuck miracle he says. In his voice I can hear lonesomeness just like mine. I want to know what happened Ole. I need to know.

I promise I will tell you. But I am waiting too.

Waiting? At your age? What the hell can you be waiting for?

A boy I say. Would you believe a boy.

I still like to do a little night fishing now and then. My house sits out on the edge of the county where the Little Missouri comes in from Montana, not too far from where my father bunked our first house all those years ago. It is about a mile and a half to the river but I know the way so well I don't bring a light. I keep a plastic bucket down there just in case I get lucky but usually it is filled with a few bottles of beer sunk in the river to keep them cold. You do have to watch out for the snapping turtles when you stick your hands into a dark river. Sometimes they clamp on to your bait and follow the line up until they're sitting in your lap.

Now this story I am about to tell I do not repeat out loud because some folks in town already think I am a crazy dinosaur. But there comes a time when you are too old to lie. On a clear night not too long ago I am sitting in my favorite fishing spot leaning back on a flat rock looking up at the stars when I sense I am not alone. This does not happen often in North Dakota. I hear something brush through the tall quackgrass right beside me too big to be a wading bird or flickerhead gopher. A prairie wolf comes down to drink. When I slowly turn my head I am staring up at an elephant. I am close enough to reach out and touch its massive leg. For a moment I wonder if I am inside another dream. Without thinking I put out my arm and rest my hand on its leg. Its skin is not what I imagine: soft and hairy. I want to speak to this magnificent animal but I do not think it speaks any of my languages. I say hello. The elephant does not pay me much attention as it dips its trunk into the river and pours the water into its mouth. Hola. When it is no longer thirsty it steps into the water without testing the depth. I guess when you are twelve feet tall you do not worry about the river being too deep. Shalom I call out. The elephant crosses the river and breaks into a run following the bottom of the ridge southwest towards the badlands. The rocks shake with the little earthquake. Hau kola! I shout in the distance. There is nothing to do but sit there and watch it go.

I come back the very next night and sit in the same place. Of course I am hoping to see an elephant again or maybe this time a giraffe or a lion. Maybe if I drink enough beer a centaur or a unicorn. As I sit in silence listening to a loon I wonder how Old Methuselah felt as he watched endless pairs of animals he had never seen before pass him by on their way to the Ark. Have you ever seen a polar bear before, wise Methuselah? Do you know what to call a platypus?

Around midnight my old eyes are growing heavy when I see something else I do not expect: a tall plume of flame coming from over the ridge. In that direction there is only the speakeasy all the children call the Sticks. Beyond that only the badlands. I wade across the shallows the water to my chest and scramble up the craggy ridge grabbing fistfuls of bindweed to steady myself as I climb the steep gorge. My legs still work. At the top I kneel down to catch my breath and look across folds of the prairie at the road house now engulfed in flames. From this distance it looks about the size of a campfire but in the white heat I can make out cars in the parking lot. The place is only a painted plywood box and it burns to the ground in a matter of minutes. Even from this distance the flames are strong enough to illuminate my face. I hear gunshots. Gunshots and what sounds like screams. Then the fire burns down and I don't hear anything. As the shadows dim I can barely make out anything in the parking lot but I think I see a car driving away. A pickup. My eyes still work. I see its headlights head off into the darkness. But it turns around after a few hundred yards and heads back. Red flashing lights on top of the truck go on and I know whose truck it is. It is a warm summer night but I shiver because I know if he finds out I am watching he will burn my house down too. The lights stop in front of the dying embers of the road house. I hear one more gunshot then silence.

I climb back down the ridge and head home. I leave my fishing gear.

I sit in my dark house and wait for sunlight. I feel so helpless the same as a hundred years ago. I know I have to tell someone. I call Annie because I only know two telephone numbers her and the young doctor and Annie has a daughter who is a state trooper. I don't know what time it is when I ring her but it must be early because she is sound asleep.

Annie I saw something last night.

You mean tonight don't you? Goddamn Ole it's still dark out.

The shack out on Weeding Road. I saw it go up in flames. I think people were killed.

I hear Annie sit up and cough. What happened? Did you ring the sheriff?

I think he might have done the killing.

Silence on the other end of the line. Okay. Okay. I'll call Louise. She'll know what to do. Damn I hope that kid Lonnie stayed home tonight. You stay put okay Ole? I'll call back.

I do not leave my house for days. Annie does not call but she comes over to tell me that Severo Rodriguez is dead.

Asshole died sitting in his truck. Ruptured something or other. Hope he burns in hell.

This was yesterday afternoon wasn't it? Around noon?

How did you know?

The day before there is a solar eclipse. Suddenly without a cloud in the sky the day goes black. I have seen them before but there are some sights you can never get used to.

I decide today is my birthday. My eyes open at dawn but I do not get out of bed right away. Something is different. I feel restless, like a boy who wakes knowing there is going to be a party that day. I lie flat with the blanket pulled up to my chin and wiggle my toes. If it is my birthday then I can eat anything I want for breakfast. Jam out of the jar. Peanut butter cookies and a cold glass of milk. Fresh strawberries with chocolate syrup.

The people from Bismarck tell me I was born in December. If I live that long I know I will get a call on the telephone from someone in Cairo or Katmandu wishing me a happy birthday. But today I feel so good I know I cannot wait that long.

I sit up in my bed. That is why I feel so different today. I wake up no longer waiting.

For the first time in a hundred years I do not dream.

Thank you thank you I whisper softly even though I am alone. Pilamaya ye.

I stand up and pace the bedroom not knowing what to do. I sit down on the bed again. A party. I run to the kitchen like a schoolboy and rifle through the drawers for anything that could be used to get ready. I do not have much experience with parties. I wonder if anyone will come. If it is Tuesday the meals on wheels lady may stop by. She will be surprised to see this old man still in his pyjamas and bare feet hanging strands of popcorn from the ceiling.

It must be around noon when Annie pokes her head in the screen door. I do not notice her I am standing on a chair looking on the top shelf for gramophone records. A party must have music I think. Music and singing. I did try the radio but something came out of the speaker that sounded like dishes being thrown on the floor. The disc jockey called it Twisted Sister.

Hey, Ole. She wipes her feet on the mat and looks around. You having a party?

It's my birthday today.

Well goddamit Ole, happy birthday. How old?

Old.

We sit in the kitchen and drink the punch I have made by combining all the leftover juice cups from my Meals on Wheels with a quart of old bootleg gin I must have hid in the pantry during prohibition.

Wow she says. This is certainly a unique flavor. She coughs.

There's apple cranberry orange grapefruit juice in there. And gin.

You don't say.

I have to push aside a few strands of popcorn to see her face. What's wrong Annie I say.

It's complicated. You remember my daughter Roxy?

Who could forget the little girl who lit the firehouse on fire.

Well she's back and she's got a new man. He's a good man, too, Ole. Good like you. They're back in Nazareth now that Severo's dead.

That doesn't sound so complicated.

Complicated part is they have a baby.

A boy.

How did you know? You been talking to Betsy? She stares down at her cup. She pushes it forward a few inches on the table. Then she pushes it back. Anyway it's complicated.

I reach out and rest my withered hand on her arm. This boy is special?

She looks me dead in the eye. That boy is a miracle. I mean it Ole. You know I never been much for religion but goddamn if I'm not ready to change because this has to be a fucking miracle. The boy saved Roxy, Ole. And I know she saved that boy, too. She loves that kid more than anything.

Annie puts both hands tight around the cup and lets out a long breath.

But the baby don't have no papers or anything you see? Kid can't grow up normal without a birth certificate. Get shots, go to school. I guess you need a doctor to fill out the right form, say they were there at the birth. But you go to the hospital and start talking to doctors and they're gonna ask questions. People wouldn't understand. Soon enough you're in jail and they take your baby away. She's that boy's mama, plain and simple. You see what I'm trying to say here Ole? You understand don't you?

I say my ears still work. And I think I can help.

You serious? She looks at me like I am selling her a lame horse. You can help?

Annie this will sound strange but I have been waiting a hundred years to help.

No bullshit.

No bullshit. Trust me. Go get Roxy and her new husband and their baby boy and come back here tonight. You can help me celebrate my birthday.

She is smiling now. She stands up from her chair and looks down at my empty table. We'll come back with a birthday cake, too. What kind you like?

Chocolate. With chocolate icing. And chocolate filling.

You sure you can handle all that?

My teeth still work.

She laughs. One triple chocolate cake coming up. And how many candles do I put on it?

One is enough.

She walks out to the porch. The weather has changed since we started talking. High clouds moving in. She opens the screen door and holds out her palm. Well Ole looks like it's gonna rain on your birthday. What time you want us to come by? Six?

Better make it eight I say. An old friend will be coming from out of town.

I watch her climb into her truck and rattle down the dirt road. I go into the living room and sit down by the telephone. I pick up the receiver and dial the only other number I know.

Hello doctor I say. I have so much to tell you.

A miracle.

Yes a miracle. Do you like chocolate cake?

I know it will be hours until they all arrive but I cannot wait. I stand outside my screen door my toes digging into the cool grass. I stick out my tongue to catch the first few drops of rain. Tonight I will eat four pieces of cake. Tonight I will ask to hold a little boy in my arms and cry tears of joy. Tonight I will sing because I feel like singing

Lord, now let your servant depart in peace
my eyes have seen salvation
Which you have prepared before the face of all people

Pilamaya ye, chinkshi. Pilamaya ye

The Finding at the Temple

Autumn 1998

Daylene had spent the first few weeks of school flipping
through the big dictionary they kept on a swivel like a gun
turret, searching for just the right word. *Bitch?* Too common.
Nemesis? Too brainy. *Whore?* Old territory. *Scumbag-sucking
Jezebel?* Too complicated, too religious.

She had been here about a month, long enough to realize
some words were never going to make it as far as Nazareth,
North Dakota. Her brother had tried to teach her some phrase
in French that sounded like *"woolee-boolee,"* but none of this
was any help at the moment because there she was, crossing
the parking lot at the SuperValu with Kathy Jubilee and her
little cronies from the Country Gals Homemaker Club dead
ahead, their pastel print dresses blowing in the warm
September breeze like flags at a theme park. Three of them
behind a table selling baked goods, which Daylene suspected
were a lot like the girls who made them: bland, with way too
much icing.

Kathy Jubilee saw her coming and fired the first shot. "Well, ladies, look at what the cathouse dragged in."

The other two, Olivia and Dagmar, covered their mouths as they laughed.

Daylene kept walking toward the automatic doors with a smile, even though inside her head there was a train wreck of words piling up: *WooleewhorescummingsuckbitchNemebel!*

She took a deep breath, stopping to look at the paper plates neatly arranged on the table. "Cupcakes. How nice," she said finally. "You girls raising money for another bus trip? Just how far is it to the abortion clinic, anyway?"

Olivia and Dagmar gasped. Kathy Jubilee silently folded her arms.

Oh, it was on.

"She's got the devil inside," Olivia said. "Someone needs to cast that devil out."

"Oh, honey," Daylene said, picking up a cupcake and then taking her sweet time to lick off the frosting. "I got about seven devils need casting." Then she put the cupcake back.

"Hey," Dagmar said. "You got to pay for that."

Daylene flipped her the bird. "You take a company check?"

She knew she'd hear about this later from Martha, when she got home. Someone's mother was bound to call and complain about the new girl destroying family values. But for the moment it was worth it. She was seventeen; it was always going to be worth it.

"That's okay, ladies," Kathy Jubilee said. "You have to take pity on the destitute."

Honestly, Daylene wasn't a hundred percent sure what the word meant, but she knew it sounded an awful lot like "prostitute," and that was enough. "Listen, blondie," she said to Kathy, leaning over the table. "One more comment from you or the other Spice Girls and I'm gonna rearrange your face, you got it?" She reached out to grab Kathy's arm, but suddenly all three girls behind the table turned their heads slightly, looking right past her.

From behind, Daylene heard someone clear their throat, a man's voice. "Any of these sugar-free?"

She turned around to face a round-faced, pudgy man wearing a brown sheriff's uniform that didn't quite fit. Great, she thought. One cop for the whole county, and he wants cupcakes.

"Why, yes sir," Kathy said, smoothing her dress and putting on a smile again. She lifted up a plate of cupcakes with glittery pink and blue frosting. "I baked these myself. How many would you like?"

"Better just make it two. I've got to watch my figure." He took a couple bills from his wallet and laid them on the table. He lowered his sunglasses to examine the short, curly-haired girl standing next to him who looked like she might spontaneously combust at any moment. "You new around here, miss?"

No answer, just an icy stare into space.

"What's your name?" he asked.

"It's Daylene Hooker," Dagmar offered quickly, her hands clasped behind her back. "Hooker, as in, you *know*."

"Yeah, she just moved here," Kathy said, handing over the cupcakes in a little paper sack. "We're kind of taking her under our wing. You know, helping her fit in."

"Well, nice to have you here, Daylene." He tipped his hat, then started back to his car.

Kathy scooped up the bills and dropped them in a tin box. "Thanks for supporting the Country Gals, Mr. Rodriguez," she called after him, adding a wave with her wrist like a beauty queen.

He slid into the open door of his sheriff's cruiser and waved back. He was probably no older than forty, but he moved like a man a lot older, rust in his joints. "You girls stay out of trouble now," he said, looking right at Daylene as he pulled out of the parking lot.

God, she missed California. Living in North Dakota gave her the feeling of being marooned on a tiny island. She had been in this town maybe a month and already she'd been told *"stay out of trouble"* a half dozen times, from teachers, supermarket checkers, old men in dusty pickup trucks, and now the sheriff. It wasn't a salutation, it was a warning; at least that's the way it seemed to Daylene.

She wasn't used to a place that had more tractors than people. Growing up an Air Force brat outside Vandyland had its drawbacks, but at least it had always been easy to become translucent to the rest of the world; unless she was bleeding or calling from county lockup, life in the Santa Barbara suburbs had been pretty much a lesson in invisibility. Sure, Cabrillo High had its share of Kathy Jubilees, but at least you could avoid them. Here, she had nineteen kids in her entire high school class, and at the moment three of them wanted to shove a cupcake up her nose.

A couple more cars had pulled up, and now there was a little line forming out into the parking lot behind Daylene, who hadn't budged from in front of the table. She realized her hands were sore from clenching into fists for so long.

"Sorry you can't afford the cupcake you ate," Kathy said after her with a pouty face. "Tell you what, it's on the house. The Country Gals care about all God's creatures great and small, don't we ladies?"

"That's right," Olivia said. "Especially the small."

Inside the SuperValu, the AC was cranked like a morgue. Daylene motored up and down all six aisles like a locomotive on rails. She stopped in front of the deli counter, trying to remember why the hell she came to the store in the first place.

She was about to walk back out when a pimply boy in a paper hat leaned on his arms from behind the counter.

"Can I help you find something?" he asked.

She turned and glared at him, storm clouds behind her eyes. "How about a stun gun."

"Don't have that," he said. "But the ground beef is in the shape of the Starship *Enterprise*, if that helps any."

She wasn't really listening. She could use a cigarette. "Wait," she said, turning to face him. "It's shaped like what?"

"You know, the Enterprise? *Star Trek?*"

Sure enough, she peered down into the glass, and there was a long aluminum tray covered with a weird topography of red meat.

The boy shrugged. "I don't eat meat myself, but it's fun to play with. Gets boring back here, you know? You should have been here last week. I made the ham salad kind of look like Captain Picard."

"You are one weird kid." She studied his face more closely now; he looked familiar.

"Mr. Deegan's class," he said. "We built a carbon dioxide molecule together."

"Oh, right." She found herself looking through her bag for a pack of smokes. "How did we do, by the way?"

"I think he gave us a C, because we made carbon *monoxide*. He said we poisoned the whole room. But at least we poisoned everyone without them knowing, on account it's odorless."

Her eyes drifted to the front doors. "I could use some of that right now."

A cart nudged in next to Daylene. The woman behind it bent over on her forearms with a weary smile, her eyes only half-open. "Hey, Jan," she said in a tired voice. "How's your mom?"

The boy's face turned pink; for most boys, talking about their mother in front of a girl was going to be an instant embarrassment. His posture stiffened, and he cleared his throat. "She's doing well, thanks. What can I get you, Aunt Roxy?"

Roxy now noticed the pretty girl with the curly dark hair standing beside her, and suddenly she realized she'd blundered into the middle of a high school crush. She ordered a pound of the fresh ground beef and smiled at Daylene, her eyes still soft and warm but becoming sharper. "I like your tattoo a lot," she said, pointing at the cookie monster on Daylene's wrist. "So, are you friends with my favorite nephew Jan here?"

Before the girl could get a word out, Jan piped up. "We made a molecule together."

Roxy shot Daylene a look of mock scandal, slapping a hand to her forehead as if she were about to faint. "Now *that* sounds like fun. Did you offer her a cigarette after, at least?"

Daylene laughed out loud; this lady was all right. And for that moment, she found herself hoping North Dakota wasn't going to be completely impossible after all. All the women she'd seen around this town were built like bars of soap; Roxy looked out of place in her cutoff jeans and ball cap, with her freckles and sun-streaked long hair and sense of humor. She seemed to be completely comfortable in her own skin.

Now if Daylene could only remember what she needed from the store in the first place, her day might officially be on the way to recovery.

Oh, yeah. Laz and his fucking Fruit Loops.

But Daylene wasn't about to let her guard down. After all, she still had to pass back through the gauntlet of Country Gals waiting outside.

Anton Rodriguez sat in his cruiser watching Lonnie's double-wide burn to the ground. He remembered a joke his father used to tell.

What kind of wood do they use to build trailer homes?
Firewood.

Anton had become used to the old ghost of Severo Rodriguez showing up uninvited.

He thought he'd parked far enough from the blaze to escape the heat, but even through the windshield he could feel it on his face, sweat beginning to bead on his forehead. There was really nothing to be done here: another lonely trailer burned down to cinders in the Badlands. He didn't know if that fool Lonnie was inside, and he didn't care. Anton just sat and watched the flames dance. Even now, the sight of an open flame—campfires, brush burns, even tiki torches at a barbecue—hauled him back to that night at the Sticks fifteen years ago. That night had forever turned him into a moth, blindly drawn towards fire as if it held some long-forgotten secret about the brother he sorely missed, or the childhood he had instantly lost.

He was hungry, but all he had in the car were the two cans of Slim Fast that Ingrid had made him take out of the fridge that morning. *Chocolate, my ass.* More like drinking cans of cold dirt. The woman meant well, but at thirty-two he was already sick of diets. He found himself growing sick of most things, actually: this job, this town, strangers, friends—if he could truly call anyone around these parts a friend. Anton had never bought into the illusion he'd be anything close to a good sheriff for Galilee County, but lately even the illusion was becoming painful. He did his job the way he followed diets, with only a smear of interest scraped too thin over a black, burnt slab of contempt and indifference. Anton thought about his father; had the Old Bear found himself tilting over the same slope sixty-odd years ago? Was it even a choice to pull back, or let fall?

He wrestled his body out of the car as the last glow of the sun disappeared beyond the far butte. In the distance he could make out Lonnie's skinny frame, a skeleton draped only in ratty underwear, drifting in between the scrub brush. He had a bottle in his hand. As Anton watched him stumble closer he thought about the crazy logic of methamphetamine: when the house is on fire, take the booze, but leave the pants. Anton sighed; now that Lonnie was alive he'd probably have to go through the trouble of arresting him. He lifted his pudgy frame out of the car and leaned his arms on the door.

"Let me guess, Lonnie," he called out. "You been cooking again?"

Lonnie shrugged his shoulders. "Man's got to make a living," he said, coming closer. "I was being real careful this time, too."

"And now you burnt your house down."

"Ain't my house," he said, smiling. "Bank foreclosed last month, remember sheriff?"

Anton nodded. "Actually, you did me a favor. Couple more months squatting, and I'd have to burn you out of this dump myself." He'd been out here a couple times to serve an eviction notice, but Lonnie would just hop on that ancient dirt bike of his and ride off into the Badlands. A padlock on the door hadn't mattered much; the walls were so thin you could punch a hole and climb through anyplace you please.

Lonnie sat down on a flat rock, his back to Anton. "I must be in the front row." Then he got quiet; it sounded like he was mumbling something to himself. He stared up at the flames in the darkening sky like a drive-in movie. "This remind you of anything, Li'l Bear?" he said, taking a pull of whiskey. "The night, I mean."

The old name surprised Anton like a hornet sting. "What did you say?"

"*Lee-tull* Bear," Lonnie said again, his back still turned, lilting the words as if reciting a faery tale to children. Then he twisted around to look at Anton, the glow of the fire reflecting off his eyes like twin dancers. "I was there, too, you know."

"Oh, yeah? And where is that?"

"Don't play dumb, Little Bear. I saw that place go up. I saw you and your old man outside."

"Stop calling me that," Anton said. "I was just a boy back then."

Lonnie spat into the dirt. "Yeah, me too, brother," he said, laughing and shaking his head. "Me too." His gaze drifted back to the fire, which had started to burn down, the whole structure now a blackened carcass of plywood. "Annie died last night, did you know that? Good old Annie. Died in her bed, at least."

"I heard about it. Guess we all got to go sometime."

Lonnie laughed again. "Oh, you're right about that, sheriff. We all got to go." He drank the rest of the bottle down, tossing it into the brush. "You've done all right for yourself, sheriff, haven't you? You even married your brother's girl. I call that all right. You probably don't remember, but I used to be friendly with Ingrid back then, too. Damn, I miss being nineteen. Those were the great times, weren't they?"

"That's enough."

"Yeah. Those were the great times. Me and Ingrid on the Ferris wheel." He spat into the ground. "Sucks to get old." He raised the bottle in some kind of toast and belched. "That's why I went out to the Sticks that night, you know. I was going to tell Ingrid, *it's either him or me.* But I guess it was neither, huh, Li'l Bear? Your papa fixed that."

"Damn it, I said that's enough."

"What are you going to do, Li'l Bear? Huff and puff and burn my fucking house down?"

"Listen, druggie, I'm warning you."

"You going to arrest me? Sounds good," Lonnie said, stumbling to his feet and moving slowly towards the cruiser. "What are we having for dinner down at the courthouse? Damn, I'm getting hungry. Hope it's pork chops. Pork chops and applesauce."

"You're pathetic," Anton said. "Get away from the car."

"And to think I remember you when you couldn't even keep your own pants up. You still remember those days, don't you, Little Bear?"

It was a reflex seldom used: Anton pulled his gun from its holster and pointed it straight at Lonnie's nose. "Damn it, I said don't call me that." He surprised himself more than anyone, but Lonnie had poked around and found a raw nerve.

"Go ahead," Lonnie said, smacking his bare chest. "Go ahead and shoot me."

The barrel trembled with Anton's hand.

Lonnie stepped forward. "Pull the trigger, Little Bear." Now both hands were on the hood of the car. "Do it. I *want* you to do it."

Now Anton's voice started to tremble along with the gun. "No one would give a damn if you die out here, you understand?"

"Shoot me."

"People'd thank me for getting rid of you. They would. Just another meth head."

"*Shoot me.*"

Anton cursed and lowered the pistol to his side. He ducked into the car and tossed it on the seat beside him, then revved the motor and turned the big Ford sedan toward the dirt track that led back to town.

Lonnie was following the car on bare feet, whooping and waving his arms around like a pale banshee glowing in the tail lights and the dying fire. Anton stopped the car. He could still back over that stick-figure son of a bitch without anyone knowing or caring. The Badlands had claimed its share of wasted lives. His hand hovered over the gear shift as he stared into the rearview at the pallid wraith dancing behind him.

Just buzzards and prairie wolves out here. Buzzards and ants.

He cursed again and jammed his foot on the gas, speeding away, rocks and red dust kicking up behind him, old ghosts swirling in his wake.

Laz watched his sister stomp up the sidewalk to the front porch, a flattened box of Fruit Loops tucked under her arm. There was chocolate smeared all over the front of her t-shirt; at least he hoped it was chocolate. "What the hell happened to you?" he said, not getting up from his chair. He pushed the brim of his hat up on his forehead and whistled. "Is that a cupcake in your hair?"

"Here's your stupid fucking cereal," she said, slinging the box at him like a Frisbee. It banged into the screen door a few inches from his head and clattered to the floor.

"Hey, watch the chapeau." He lifted the crumpled box to his ear and shook; it sounded like sand inside. "Did you tell them off in French, like I told you? *Poulet moulet.* Literally it means 'wet chicken.' It's like, the worst possible thing you could say to a French person."

"Yeah well, we're not in France, Laz. Far as I can tell we're not anywhere." She started to pry bits of cupcake from her head, tossing them into the weeds that were in complete control of their little front yard. It stuck to her dark curls like plaster. "And not in a million years would I call someone a wet chicken."

"Suit yourself," he said, smoothing a wrinkle in his shirt. "*Quelle dommage.*"

She stood over him, glaring as he sagged back against the wall. She scraped the bottom of her shoe back and forth against the floorboards as if trying to spark a fire under his chair. This was the one situation where big brothers were supposed to come in handy. Most of the time they were better off being invisible, but now they were supposed to go out and find the creeps and then say things like "*You messin' with my little sister, you messin' with me!*" or "*If I catch you even lookin' at her funny, I'll kick your ugly face in!*" while they held them up against a wall. Big brothers weren't supposed to just sit on the porch and spout French. Laz had many qualities she was glad for, but temporary bouts of blind rage would never be one of them. Still, she was pissed. He could at least *act* like he gave a damn.

"Aren't you supposed to be mowing the lawn or something, instead of just sitting out here?" Daylene asked. "Mom should be home soon."

"The major won't be back until Monday, maybe Tuesday," he said. "She called while you were being outgunned at the Cupcake Corral."

Daylene's foot stopped. "Mom called?" she said, her voice softening and showing a few cracks. "What did she say?"

He looked down the street, clearing his throat. "Let's see. Big project, blah blah blah. National security, blah blah blah. Won't be home until Monday or Tuesday, blah blah blah. Tell Martha to break into the kangaroo and buy the groceries, blah blah blah. Tell Daylene to learn how to dodge cupcakes better, blah blah blah. That about covers it."

For once, Daylene wished he would fill in the "blah blah blahs."

Martha burst out onto the porch, holding the ceramic kangaroo where they always kept the emergency money.

"It's empty," she said, holding it upside down and shaking it. "Laz, I'm not even going to ask this time."

"We keep money in there?" he said, eyes wide with mock disbelief. "I always thought it was cookies."

Martha was about to make Laz empty his pockets—it wouldn't be the first time—but she noticed the fudgy disaster that resembled her little sister and stopped cold. "What happened to you?"

Daylene tilted her head to one side. "I slipped."

"She had a fight with Willie Wonka," Laz said. "I think she lost."

Daylene snarled and swung for his nose. Laz slipped the punch but leaned too far, tipping his chair and landing on the hardwood with a dull thud. His hat flew off and rolled into a corner.

Daylene stood over her brother. "Sometimes you're a real asshole, Laz."

Martha moved to get between them, but Daylene had already turned and bulled her way inside, slamming the screen door and heading for the upstairs bathroom. From the porch, Martha and Laz could hear the bathroom door bang shut and then lock behind her. Then the shower running, hot water slowly building to make the house's ancient plumbing shudder and scream. Then the CD player in the shower, turned all the way up on a song they'd heard too many times before. Then Daylene's banshee voice, trying to sing along.

"Sarah McLachlan," Martha said. "This must be serious."

Laz got up and dusted himself off. "We need to buy that girl singing lessons before she kills somebody."

Martha scowled at him. "She needs someone to stick up for her, not poke fun."

"Well, I'll leave that to you, Mrs. Hooker," he said, lifting his shoe up on the rail and rubbing a smudge from the toe with the palm of his hand. "I'm off." He fixed his hat, running his fingers along the brim.

Martha put down the jar and grabbed his shoulders, pushing him against the wall. They were about the same height and weight, but she had always been stronger. "Give me the money, Laz."

He frowned. "How do you know Daylene didn't take it? Or coyotes? I hear the coyotes around here will steal just about anything: babies, money, unlocked cars."

Martha closed her eyes and let out a long, weary sigh. "Around here, I think they call them prairie wolves. And enough with the jokes. I know what you're doing with the money, all right? I know," she said, her voice lowering to a whisper. "I just don't want Daylene to know. She's got enough problems without finding out her brother is a drug addict."

"That's harsh," he said, recoiling from her touch. "I'm having a little fun, is all."

"Just keep your *fun* away from Daylene and this house, all right?" She waited until his eyes rose to meet hers. "Now, the money," she said, her hand out.

He groaned as he reached into his trouser pocket and handed over a thin wad of bills. "I was going to have a great weekend with that." He looked up and down the empty street. "If my ride ever shows up, that is."

"Your source, you mean," she said. "Or whatever you call it."

He laughed. "My *source*? Damn, sis, you've been watching too much *Law & Order*."

"Well, I do have a crush on Jerry Orbach," she said. "But I'm serious about this, Laz. You need to get some help."

He stood up, brushing off his fedora. "Let me get this straight, Nancy Reagan," he said, starting down the steps and onto the sidewalk. "You have a crush on Jerry Orbach, and you say *I* need help?" With that, he cocked the hat stylishly on his head, striding as if he suddenly found himself on Hollywood Boulevard.

"You're going to stick out around here, wearing stuff like that," she called after him.

"Ain't that the truth," he said, not turning around.

Martha leaned her head against the porch rail and watched him disappear down the sidewalk, shaking her head at the hat, the silk shirt, the creased pants, the wingtip shoes. The outfit could use a walking stick; she figured at least he'd have something to defend himself with when the locals tried to run him down with their pickup trucks.

She checked her watch and tried to remember where she'd left the keys to the Subaru. The SuperValu would close in an hour, along with the rest of this town. She made a note to run the push mower over the yard when she got back; it wasn't like Laz was ever going to get around to doing it. She had to remind herself that he was her older brother, by almost three years.

She picked up the fallen chair and put it back in its place. This porch needed a good sweep and mop. So what if she had a crush on Jerry Orbach? On TV he seemed like the only nice person in an entire metropolis of creeps and strangers.

Through the upstairs window, she could hear the shower trickle to a stop. Daylene would be ready to talk to her now; Martha would stop by the kitchen for a couple of Klondike bars before going upstairs to knock lightly on her sister's bedroom door.

On the way inside the house she caught her reflection in the enormous hall mirror that stood like a sentinel beside the stairs. She hated making eye contact with her own reflection; she avoided looking at herself except in the dimmest of light. Alone now, she leaned her hand on the banister and raised her eyes to take a long look at herself in the dusty mirror. God, she looked like a housewife: soiled apron on top of a bulky flower-print dress, house shoes, straw-colored hair tied down under a blue bandana like a loose haystack. Even her eyeglasses were for an old woman. She acted like one, too, clipping coupons, doing the laundry, even checking Daylene's math homework after making dinner. But she wasn't a housewife, merely the daughter of a woman who was out inspecting missile silos. Most days it didn't bother her—she liked losing herself to routines, having people depend on her—but some days Martha yearned to simply be a girl again, meeting friends at the movies, looking at college brochures, riding in cars with boys. She broke her gaze and went into the kitchen, opening the freezer.

"Martha?" her sister's voice called from the top of the stairs. "You still here?"

"Be right up," she called, stopping in front of the mirror once more to stare at the old woman trapped behind the glass. Then she headed up the creaky steps, ice cream already melting in her hand.

Midnight in Nazareth. Lonnie naked in the Badlands. Naked like a baby except for shoes. *Lost* would be too kind a description. Stopping to rest on a bald rock, raw hands checking the darkness for snakes. Wondering how far he will be from the cemetery when the sun decides to come up. Two days on foot? On *his* feet, maybe three. Never make it. Managing a chuckle: *what to wear, what to wear.*

Lying down silently, waiting. Listening to the prairie wolves mourn.

"Shame this is the only time we get to see everybody," Betsy said. "Weddings and funerals."

Roxy nodded, her head turned to the dirty window as she peered out at the grey sky. It was still September, but she could swear it was about to snow. That morning had been cold enough to make the grass at the cemetery crunch under her feet, heavy with frozen dew. But that was autumn in North Dakota: a month or two of short, warm days wedged in between the chilled sprawl of night. Only a few more weeks and there'd be chains on tires.

Roxy leaned back and closed her eyes, shifting uncomfortably. She had a full mug balanced on her knee, but she'd let the coffee go cold. Only now she realized she was sitting in Annie's chair; as far as easy chairs went, this one was a loser. The old green fabric had worn down to the wood and the cushion springs were shot. But not in a million years would she ever think of getting rid of it. More than anything, right now she wanted Annie to barrel out of the kitchen and tell her, "*Put a napkin under that cup, you'll stain the fabric.*" She thought of the way Annie used to wring her hands together when she was cross, like a doctor getting ready for surgery. It was an old memory; the last time she could remember Annie doing that, she and Louise had lashed Eggs to a kitchen chair in Saran wrap, pretending he was a caterpillar ready to change into a butterfly. They had danced around him while he struggled to break free of the plastic cocoon, all three chanting, "*Go, butterfly, go! Go, butterfly, go!*" Then Annie had run in and looked at her children with a pale stare as if she'd suddenly discovered little aliens inhabiting her house.

The image made Roxy smile. Annie hadn't been very old when she died, barely into her seventies, but boy—she'd sure had her share of mileage. Mostly all highway miles.

"Roxy?" Betsy said, gently jogging her arm. "Roxy, you all right?"

"Fine," she said. "If I don't get the chance, thank Zeke for the fine words."

"He'll be pleased to hear that." Betsy played with a fold of her black skirt, twisting it in both hands. "It really was a wonderful ceremony."

Roxy nodded again; she'd been doing a lot of that the last few days, moving her head or hands to communicate, more or less mute. It had been a nice ceremony, though. Annie was laid to rest just where she'd wanted, in the little graveyard overlooking the Little Missouri where they'd buried Joachim the year before. Joachim, the prodigal husband who had shown up in town one day after a lifetime of self-exile. Annie had embraced him immediately, but Roxy had thought the old man simply ran out of places to put the good book; even America can run out of motels.

Outside she could see Louise walking up the road from town, Eggs in tow behind her like a scolded child. He only had a t-shirt and sweatpants on, the bare skin of his arms almost blue; he'd probably been hanging out in the tractor graveyard again, sitting on the old machines and pretending to make them go. He'd been down there since Annie died, next to the auto shop, like he was waiting for her to get back to work. The black suit he'd worn to the funeral was probably scattered to the weeds. She knew Annie's passing would be hard on her and Louise, but it would always be harder on Eggs.

Eggs and Lonnie, too. Both of them were lost souls now.

She watched Eggs trudge inside to the porch, Louise rubbing the cold from his arms. He turned impatiently in a small circle, still her little brother even though he now was forty-odd years old, with greying hair and stubbled beard. Louise coaxed him to sit in one of the rocking chairs on the porch while she got him a hot drink. "Hot chocolate," he said too loud, making some of the people who'd been chatting in low tones turn to stare. "Marshmallows."

Right now she wanted to pray for her little brother, but she couldn't come up with the right words. As a girl, Roxy had never been much for prayers, but that had changed after moving back to Nazareth.

Hell, she thought, everything changed.

Instead of a prayer she whispered under her breath, "*Go, butterfly, go. Go, butterfly, go.*"

Her gaze followed her sister to the kitchen, where the younger cousins were hanging out, bored and waiting. Jan and Sam were standing by the cupboards together, leaning on the back counter that was already crowded with casserole dishes and cake pans that people had brought along. Just what she needed: a twelve-year supply of bundt cake.

Roxy took a minute to look both boys over; it was rare to see them side by side. They were about the same height with the same amount of tangled leather-brown hair, but everything else was different: the clothes, the facial expressions, the way they stood. Jan was animated when he spoke, his hands moving about with every word; a preacher's son, no doubt about it. He had a ragged camel-hair blazer draped over his thin frame, an old hand-me-down from his father that was, as far as Roxy knew, worn day and night. When he reached college the other kids would probably call it "vintage." His khaki slacks were a couple sizes too big, as well, rolled up at the cuffs and cinched around his waist by a thick leather belt that had been made for a much stouter man. His dress shirt still had the creases from the package, and the tie was a clip-on, uncomfortably hugging the boy's neck. Betsy had bought the shirt at Joraanstad's the day before; she'd probably had to sit on the boy to make him wear it in public.

Roxy had bought Sam a collared shirt, too, but she knew he wouldn't wear it. He stood next to Jan, leaning to one side and nodding his head slightly as he listened to his cousin talk. Now and then he'd look out the window as if waiting for someone. He had a bomber jacket with a rip down the back over the usual black t-shirt. Lee jeans worn almost down to the thread. The t-shirt gripped his chest; yes, she could see her boy had muscles. Sam had played football for the school the last couple years until he quit before the new season, after only a few practices. Something about the coach wanting him to cut his hair; that was the story Sam had given her and Joe, anyway. Yes, her boy had secrets, too. Usually it's the parents who grow too protective of their children, trying to shield them from anything too big or too strong. But with Sam it was the other way around. Sometimes he looked at Roxy and Joe like he felt sorry for them. Of course, every kid probably had the same look for their folks. But she knew Sam was always going to be different than any other kid. Every mother swears her child is special, set apart from the rest; she'd seen a bumper sticker on a minivan the other day that read *My Child can Kick Your Honor Student's Ass.* But Roxy truly wished he could grow up like any other boy, average and invisible. In her heart, she knew that was never going to happen.

Annie's death weighed on her mind, but even more burdensome was the heavy dread of knowing that sooner or later, her son would leave her, like Joachim had done all those years before. From the living room she looked at her son, studying him, determined to remember every detail about him, as if he would soon fade from her sight like an apparition. It was only a matter of time, she thought, until she looked up one day and found that he was gone. Watching them both from the living room, she didn't want to look away, for fear of missing something.

"Roxy," Betsy said, pulling on her arm again. "Your coffee's gone cold."

"Jan's shot up since the last time I saw him," Roxy said, a white lie she didn't mind telling her cousin; Betsy's son hadn't grown much in years. "He's about ready for college?"

"Ready? I think he wants to go *now*. He won't stop talking about that class trip they've got over to Bismarck next week."

"Trip?" Roxy hadn't heard anything about a class trip. But it didn't surprise her that Sam had never mentioned it; Sam, the brooding boy who had made it to seventeen without ever really mentioning anything.

"You know, to the university. They let them walk around the campus, sit in on classes and all that. Jan says he'd be happy just spending the whole time walking around in a real library." Betsy took the cup and saucer from Roxy's lap and put them on the table. "So, is Sam thinking about college?"

"Who knows what that boy is thinking about," she said. "You know Sam."

"He's just the strong and silent type is all. I can see him as an English major, or something like that. Maybe creative writing. He's going to be a famous novelist or playwright, I just know it."

"Oh, he can tell a story all right," Roxy said, tongue firmly in her cheek. She shifted in her chair, still looking out into the kitchen at the two boys. "Cousin, have you ever looked at your boy and thought, you're going to lose him? I mean, you ever get a feeling your boy is a big fish swimming around in a small pond?"

"My Jan?" Betsy said, the pitch of her voice suddenly changing, and immediately Roxy wanted to take the question back; she knew Betsy wasn't ready to think about not having her only son close by.

"I take it back," Roxy said, smiling. "Just my middle age talking out loud is all."

Betsy gave Roxy a worried look, biting her lip. "Jan seems pretty happy here, right? I mean, you don't think he's—"

Roxy leaned over to put her hand on Betsy's wrist. "Listen, anyone with half a brain can see he's a NoDak boy, just like his father."

With that, Betsy seemed satisfied, easing back a bit into the couch.

"I was really thinking about Sam," Roxy said, lowering her voice to a whisper. "Sometimes I wonder about him, that's all."

"Boys," Betsy said, trying to be helpful. "Who can figure them out?"

"Yeah," Roxy said. "Boys." Boys and men.

She looked for Joe; last time she'd seen him he was lugging grocery bags in from his truck. He had been distant these past few days, giving her the space to grieve. She loved him for that. In a moment she would find the gumption to get up out of Annie's easy chair and go look for him. Perhaps this had all been the hardest on Joe after all, she thought; he must feel like he's on the outside of all this family business. She loved the man as much as anything on this earth, even if she had forgotten to tell him that lately. She loved him as much as her own son.

Their son.

She got up, telling Betsy she wanted to find Joe and ask about this class trip business. But mostly it was an excuse to go tell him the truth: that he was her family. She wanted to tell him that she'd have never made it this far without him.

Midnight in Nazareth. Joe Davidson feeling too old to be doing this, but doing it anyway. Doing exactly what his own old man would have done after an argument: get in his truck, take a deep breath, put his seatbelt on.

Then, wait for the asshole to come out of the bar.

Listening to a call-in show from Regina on the pickup's battered radio as a distraction. Waiting. Trying to remember a time he'd started a fight with someone; not remembering any. Telling himself he should just get home and climb into bed with Rock. She's probably up, anyway. She'll be up most nights for a while, with Annie gone.

Getting out of the truck when the bar door opens. "Carl. You called my kid a retard?"

Carl putting up his hands like this is a holdup. "Now, Joe, I didn't know you were in there when I said it," he says. "I might've had a few too many Co-Colas, all right, big fella?" A few of the other men spilling out of the bar now, sensing the sudden change in weather. The new audience and the warm liquor turning in his belly making Carl more bold; he puts his hands down and hooks his thumbs in his belt. "Anyways, he ain't even your kid. Stepson don't *count*."

"He's my boy," Joe says, stepping closer. "And you called him a retard."

Joe dodging a sucker-punch too slowly, Carl's fat knuckles grazing his ear. Now Joe swinging back, Carl too drunk to play defense, Joe's canned-ham of a fist landing squarely in his floppy gut and knocking the air out of him all at once like a potato chip bag. Carl falling back on the cracked pavement as if someone jerked away his chair at the last second. Clutching at his stomach. Thinking about vomiting. But breathing.

Now Joe standing over him. "You all right?" Helping him to his feet. They would shake hands at the Rooster in the morning, mumble some words, buy each other coffee and eggs.

Joe scowling at the other men of Nazareth outside the bar. "He's my boy."

Daylene watched from her seat as Kathy Jubilee and her two flunkies boarded the bus and slithered down the aisle, weaving slowly toward her like a squadron of medusas, making eye contact with everyone they passed as if their gaze could turn flesh to stone. Right now she wasn't feeling so good about her decision to get here early to stake out the back row of seats; now it felt like a trap. And having that goofy nerd Jan next to her wasn't going to be much help, either; he was nice enough, but he wasn't the kind of kid who could repel boarders. Maybe he could talk them to death about Yoda or Klingons.

She thought about making a break for it and ditching this trip altogether. Spending three hours in a bus each way just to walk around some hokey college was bad enough, but now the thought of being stuck on the same bus as the three sirens made her stomach churn. She suddenly felt short of breath, her skin hot and clammy; she needed some air. She tried to crack the window, but it wasn't the kind that opened.

She slipped off her jacket. *Climate control, my ass.*

Before she knew it, Kathy was standing over her and Jan, a smile spreading across her face like a crocodile. And just like that, it was on again.

"Well, look at this beautiful couple hiding out in the back, ladies," Kathy said, smacking her gum and shaking her head. "Talk about opposites attract."

"Preacher Boy and Hooker Girl," Olivia said. "Sounds like a comic book."

"Sounds like a porno," Dagmar said. "Starring a bonafide *Hooker*, even."

"Just ignore them," Jan whispered. "I've gotten good at that."

"Hey, Daylene, I've been meaning to ask you," Olivia said. "What's the best way to get chocolate out of your hair?"

"Let me show you," Daylene said, whipping her jacket at the girl. She'd already climbed halfway over Jan's legs when an unfamiliar voice came from behind the Country Gals.

"Hey, cousin," Sam said, slipping through the crowded aisle. "Change seats with me, will you? I got one up front next to Coach Bott, and you know I can't spend three hours sitting next to that guy." He bent to pick up Daylene's windbreaker from the floor. "Is this yours?"

"Hey, Sam," Kathy said, actually flipping her hair as she said it. "You don't want to sit next to this one. She's got problems."

As Daylene reached out she felt a hand on her shoulder, firmly pushing her back. It was Sam, of course, but his touch surprised her more than anything. Something electric happened when he touched her, she was sure of it. She sat back down.

Sam smiled at Kathy. "Problems? That's not what I heard."

"Oh really? And what did you hear?" Kathy drew back a step, folding her arms.

"About this girl? I heard she's deadly with a cupcake. I mean, deadly like a *ninja*." With his free arm he cocked back and threw an imaginary fastball toward the front of the bus. "Matter of fact, did you hear that she got ambushed outside the SuperValu a couple weeks ago? Yeah, outnumbered three to one, but she still managed to kick ass. And I think there's even pictures to prove it," he said, sitting up a bit. "Hey, Jan, didn't you say you took pictures?"

Jan was already halfway down the aisle, looking for a new place to sit. "Pictures?"

Coach Bott's grizzled voice came on the PA. "*All right, everyone find a seat.*"

Kathy didn't budge, still smacking her gum. Olivia and Dagmar stood behind her, not breaking formation.

"*That means you, ladies.*"

Finally, the Country Gals melted backwards, sliding quietly into seats a few rows up.

"Thanks," Daylene said, surprised Sam knew about the cupcake fiasco.

"What for?"

"You know," she said. "For keeping me from killing that girl."

"Don't underestimate her," he said. "Kathy's pretty tough. She's got a great left hook."

"How do you know that?"

He shrugged. "She's my girlfriend."

She felt the blood drain from her face. "You go out with Kathy Jubilee."

"Hey, I'm human." Sam rummaged through his backpack and pulled out a battered CD player and untangled the headphones. "You like metal?" he said to her, but Daylene had already turned her entire body to stare out the window. That touch of his hand was already a cold memory.

"Hey, I was kidding, you know."

She turned back. "What, about being human?"

"About me and Kathy," he said, starting to laugh. "Not my type."

She turned back around. "Just what is your type, then?"

He shrugged. "I got a weakness for ninjas."

Now they both laughed. Daylene karate-chopped the felt seat-back a little too hard, making the kid sitting in front of her turn around and give them both an annoyed look. She realized she'd never even seen Sam smile before, let alone laugh. After a few minutes the bus pulled onto the highway; now there was nothing to see except blank horizon until they reached the other end of North Dakota. But she acted like she was interested anyway, picking a rock or piece of scrub and concentrating on it with her eyes until it was past them. She wanted to keep this conversation going, so she scanned her brain for small talk. "So, you thinking about college?"

"What for," he said, looking past her at the vast flatness passing their window. "They ain't going to teach me anything." Sam put his headphones on and rocked his head with the music, his eyes closed.

Joe slowed down as the truck reached the far edge of town, its bed squeaking like an old mattress with every bump as the road turned from smooth asphalt to red dirt and gravel. James was slumped in the passenger seat, heavy eyes fluctuating between full and crescent moons, empty lunchbox cradled in his lap like a sleeping baby.

They had been getting home late the last couple weeks, the job site an hour away at the southern lip of the county. There was no adventure in putting up a plywood fast-food joint across the street from the Rodriguez Outlet Mall, but paid work was paid work. They needed the money. Another month and it would be too cold for any real carpentry jobs; *Joseph Davidson & Sons* would have to get by doing indoor add-ons and emergency roofing calls until April, when the ground thawed again.

As he made the turn off the main road he noticed a girl he hadn't seen before in front of their place, standing out by the battered mailbox. Then things got a little more strange: when he pulled into the driveway there was a sheriff's cruiser parked in front of the house. James jerked up in his seat, eyes wide now as he looked around the yard. He had his door open before the truck stopped.

"Easy," Joe said to him, putting it in park. "Could be nothing."

He saw Roxy standing on the porch and could tell by the sour look on her face that it wasn't going to be nothing. She had her arms folded, her foot tapping a hole into the floor. Two men were on the steps, leaning on the railing and looking up at her like a pair of suitors. He recognized Anton Rodriguez right away, but he had to get closer to make out the other as the football coach, another rotund man, with a sheepdog look hanging on his stubbled face.

"Evening," Joe said as he came up, putting his own foot up on the porch steps.

"They left Sam in Bismarck," Roxy said. "They just left him there. He could be dead in a dumpster, and nobody seems to give a damn."

Coach Bott backed up a step, his voice cracking. "Ma'am, I've been at the school for going on thirty years now. When a kid gets lost, that's one thing; we'll find him. But when a kid doesn't want to be found? That's another." He turned to Joe. "I'm telling you we looked everywhere, Mr. Davidson. Bismarck ain't New York City, y'know. Sooner or later we had to get the rest of those kids back home."

"You know how Sam is, Joe," Anton interrupted.

Roxy's voice was now somewhere in the stratosphere. "Oh, and how is that, sheriff?"

"Well, he hangs around with some unsavory types," the sheriff replied, his fingers smoothing the brim of his hat. "You could say he's got a reputation for being a mite difficult."

"I don't believe this," she said, throwing her arms up. "You're not going to do anything?"

Joe stood silently at the bottom of the steps, listening and watching.

"Nothing to do," Anton said, putting his hat back on. "He's a big boy, almost eighteen. Come on, Roy," he said to the coach, whose head was bowed as the two men ambled away. "If I do hear anything," Anton called back to the porch, "I'll be sure to let you know."

Joe had been silent all this time, taking everything in. But now as they turned back to their car he followed them, towering over both men in the growing darkness. "One thing," Joe said, putting his hand on the passenger door, preventing the coach from opening it. He spoke softly, making sure Roxy and James couldn't hear from the house. "If anything happens to that boy, I'm going to come find you," he said, his voice low and calm, like a teacher giving simple instructions before an exam. "Both of you. Do you understand?"

Anton tried to laugh, but the nervous chuckle only trickled off his lips. "Now, Mr. Davidson, you're not threatening your local sheriff, are you?" It was something his father, Severo, might have said, but from Anton's mouth it was only a pale imitation, an obvious fake.

Joe leaned over the hood. "Listen close: I don't care if you're Moses and this asshole is Mother Teresa. Anything happens to my son, and I'm coming back for you. Period." Joe took his hand off the door and turned back to the house, his wide shoulders tensed.

Roxy was crying now, pacing in crazy circles on the porch like a broken toy. James was up on the steps, watching his father's face in the dim light for any clues. Joe watched the police cruiser back around the truck and disappear down the road.

"If you're going to look for Sam," James said, "I'm coming with you."

"Someone's got to stay by the telephone," Joe said, running a hand under his ball cap. "And looking at your mother here, I'm guessing she's not going to volunteer." He trudged up the steps and put his hands around her shoulders. "Come on," he said, pushing her gently in the direction of the truck. "Let's go."

"I guess I always knew he was going to leave us," she said, wiping tears from her face. "I just didn't think it would be so soon."

"Don't say that, Rock. We don't know for sure," he said, leaning across her and putting on her seatbelt for her. "Kids stray off all the time. You remember back in Cairo when James decided to run away? Came back after a few hours when he was hungry."

She looked at him. "You know what I'm talking about."

"Yeah," he said, not returning her stare. "I know." He got back in and turned the truck around on the grass. They headed back toward the road. As they reached the mailbox, they both noticed the short girl standing there, hands dug deep into her black leather jacket.

"Hey, stop," Roxy said, rolling down her window. "I know that girl. Stop the truck."

Joe rolled to a gentle stop in front of the girl and killed the engine.

"Hey," Roxy said. "Daylene, right? Did you go on that class trip today?"

The girl nodded slowly, her head cocked to one side. "You going to fetch Sam?"

"You bet," Roxy said. "You have any clue about where he might be?"

Daylene kicked lightly at the mailbox post with her sneaker a few times before she said anything. "Well, me and him spent the whole day together, going from classroom to classroom. He wanted to talk to all the professors," she said. "It was kind of weird."

Roxy and Joe looked at each other, giving each other a knowing nod. "Thanks, Daylene," Roxy said. "Can we give you a ride back to your house? Your folks might be worried."

"They ain't," Daylene said quickly, pulling out a hand and pointing back towards town. "I live right there on Main Street, just a few houses down." She dug her hands into her jacket. There was a restlessness to her body, as if it was moving in a thousand directions while still standing in place. She bit her lip. "I hope you find him."

Joe leaned over the wheel and patted the dashboard with his big hand. "Don't worry, Daylene, we'll find him. This old truck is part hound dog." He started it again.

Roxy waved to Daylene as the truck pulled slowly onto the main road and lumbered back to town, toward the state highway. In the rearview they both watched the curly-haired girl start on the quarter mile back to town.

"You mean it *smells* like a hound dog," Roxy muttered, gulping air from the open window as they picked up speed. "Damn, Joe, what died in here?"

"Ah, *there's* the sweethearted devil we all love," he said, reaching over to gently rub the back of his wife's long neck. "Welcome back, lover."

"Whatever. How fast can the hound dog get us to Bismarck?"

"Maybe two-and-a-half hours, with no traffic."

"This is North Dakota," she said, settling into her seat. "There's no traffic."

As they neared the Kum n' Go that sat on the edge of the dusty highway, Joe looked at the gas gauge and clicked his teeth. He pulled the hound dog up beside the lone pump. "We got time for a coffee? Maybe even a Danish?"

She nodded; she'd forgotten the poor man hadn't had dinner yet.

Roxy elected to pump the gas while Joe went inside to pay and get snacks. He looked into his wallet. "Put twenty in, that'll be enough to get us to Bismarck."

As she leaned against the high bed of the truck and looked around, her eye caught on the three guys standing on the side of the cinder-block gas station, smoking cigarettes and drinking out of paper bags. *Unsavory types.* One of them seemed woefully out of place, though, with strange clothes and a fancy hat that made him look like some kind of private eye in those old black-and-white movies where a girl with a black veil raps on the glass door. She wondered if any of these guys were friends with Sam; at that moment she realized she had no idea if her boy even had friends. A deep chill suddenly ran up her back. She felt it in her teeth. Roxy finished filling the truck and hustled back into the cab.

The first half-hour of their trip was silent, Joe munching on powdered donuts while Roxy lost herself in her thoughts. The air was getting cold, and she rolled the window up. Joe thought about turning on the radio to help keep himself awake, but he started humming under his breath instead.

"Hey, Joe," she said, blowing on her coffee. "Do you think Sam and Daylene—I mean—"

"Well, let's look at the facts: she doesn't talk much, and she thinks he's 'kinda weird.' Sounds like a match to me."

"I'm such a bad mother," she said. "I don't even know if he has a girlfriend, or if he's got *friends*, period. He's seventeen, and I don't know shit about him."

Joe jerked the wheel and pulled off onto the loose gravel on the side of the road. The truck bounced to a stop in the dirt. Roxy held on to the doorframe, hair tousled now and covering her eyes. "What are you doing?"

"Listen," he said, turning off the ignition. "You're a good mother. Wait. Fuck that, you're a *great* mother. Not just for Sam, but for Lydia and James too. You understand?"

"If I'm such a great mother, why am I driving across the state to find my son?"

"You know why," he said. They were alone for miles on the deserted highway, but still his voice lowered to a whisper, burdened by secrets. "He's got to find his own way."

"So he disappears, just like that?" Her hands took flight. "I didn't sign up for this, Joe. Damn it, I'm his *mother*."

"He doesn't want to hurt you," he said. "But he knows he will."

They sat like that for a while, cold creeping into the cab until they could see their breath dance in the spotted moonlight. Every few minutes a pair of headlights would show on the horizon.

"You're a great mother because you're there when he needs you. Yeah, it's a shitty job," he said, finding her hand in the dark. "You feel like you're not worth as much as you used to be. Hell, I miss Lydia every single day. And I know James isn't going to stick around forever. But when they leave, it doesn't mean they love me any less. It just means they have to find their own way." He took a deep breath. "I didn't know you as a young girl, but I've heard stories, and if I had to guess I'd say Annie had her hands full with you. When you up and left her, she must've gone crazy with all that waiting. Hell, I know it sucks. But right now, it's all you can do."

She rubbed her runny nose, a tiny smile sprouting on her lips. "I *was* a bit of a wildcat," she said, her voice now raspy with old tears. She caught her pale reflection in the rearview mirror. "God, I feel so old, Joe. I feel like a worn shoe."

"Well, you look amazing to me," he said, starting the truck again. "And trust me, you're still one hell of a wildcat." They kissed, and Joe pulled them back onto the blacktop, picking up speed as the truck rattled east toward the county line.

"Joe," she said, reaching over and grabbing his near hand from the steering wheel, bringing it to her face. "Thanks." His rough skin felt warm on her cheek. She moved closer, leaning her head on his shoulder, the sawdust on his jacket making her nose twitch. "Your truck still smells, though."

A few more miles and they would turn south, cutting across North Dakota's empty back roads until they reached eighty-three, the four-lane expressway that ran north-south from Minot down to Bismarck. Roxy worked the knobs on the truck's ancient radio and found Bruce Springsteen singing "Darlington County." They hadn't heard it in years, but they sang the words they knew. Suddenly they were back in Cairo, parking on a deserted stretch of the levee and watching the grain barges slip south along the Mississippi in the night.

"Come on and take a seat on my fender," Joe sang along, about as off-key as any human being could get.

She reached over and put her hand over his mouth. "I love you," she said, actually managing a laugh. "You can't sing worth a damn, but I love you."

Together they rolled along the twisting highway, a mother and father in search of a son.

Midnight in Nazareth. Daylene on the front porch, smoking the last of her brother's store-boughts. Wondering what those pills next to his badly hidden stash of weed would turn out to be. She has an idea, but she won't ask. Waiting for headlights to turn off the empty highway and head into Nazareth. Can't sleep anyway. Watching her chilled breath drift away and disappear into the night. They would have to pass by her house on the way home. She would look for him in the window as the truck passed, maybe offer him a wave.

Maybe a karate chop.

Roxy and Joe followed the sleepy tide of students shuffling to their 8:00 a.m. classes. Joe felt like he was walking around a lost city, or maybe the moon; all the grass and statues and trimmed hedges made him feel like he'd snuck into a private park without permission. The only time he'd set foot on a college before was to see Lydia graduate last year in Minneapolis, but that was different: they had been expecting visitors.

They had been in the truck all night, crisscrossing the small grid of Bismarck streets that hugged either side of Interstate 94, hoping to get lucky. They leaned against a bronze statue of a bison and drank their fifth cups of gas station coffee while students shelled in heavy jackets and backpacks filed past like zombies into a lecture hall.

Roxy mustered a weary smile. "Well, old man, you ready to go to college?"

"Long as I don't have to eat goldfish," he said. "Or sleep with a goat."

They must have ducked their heads into thirty classrooms in three different buildings. Finally, Joe thought he heard the boy's voice coming from behind a door. It was a large lecture hall, with a steep cone of desks leading down to a round floor. And sure enough, there was a kid who looked a lot like Sam at the bottom, sitting across a table from an old man who looked exactly the way Joe had pictured a college professor: big glasses, bald head, even the funny jacket with patches on the sleeves. All that was missing was a pipe.

The kid talking to him was Sam, all right.

Joe ducked his head back out into the hallway and motioned for Roxy, and together they went in and stood at the top circle of desks to listen to the heated conversation between the professor and their seventeen-year-old boy from Nazareth. It wasn't exactly clear what they were arguing about, but whatever the subject, Joe and Roxy knew it was over their head. History? Philosophy, maybe. The twenty or so students scattered around the cavernous hall watched intently, some scribbling notes.

Joe whispered over to a student sitting in the back row, a kid with a moon-shaped face and glasses covered halfway with shaggy drapes of morning hair. "Hey, buddy—what class is this?"

"Senior seminar in Ethics," the kid said, not looking up from his notebook. He jabbed his pen at the notes he'd been taking. "This is great stuff."

"Hey," Roxy called out, suddenly remembering she was a mother who had just spent dusk until dawn scouring the streets of Bismarck for this boy. She had the right to be mad. "Excuse me," she said again, cupping her hands around her mouth to make her voice echo throughout the room. "Hey, down there. Remember me? Your mother?" Everyone turned to look at her; there were a few giggles. She was hoping Sam would look up at her with a look of surprise and shame, a boy embarrassed by his mother. But he didn't look up at all.

Joe took a few of the steps slowly. "Let's go home, son," he said in his calm voice. He looked around at all the students who were now staring at him, making him uncomfortable in the sudden spotlight. "Come on. We don't belong here."

The professor who had been sitting across from Sam as they talked stood up from his chair. "Wait a minute," he said, scratching his bald head. "You don't even go to school here?"

"He's a junior in high school," Roxy said, folding her arms. "And he's currently AWOL."

The moon-faced boy nudged a girl sitting next to him. "This is just like that movie *Good Will Hunting*," he said, still writing furiously in his notebook. "Only now, Matt Damon is in high school. Awesome, man. Awesome."

Now the professor looked more closely at the boy sitting across from him. The whole classroom fell silent. Without a word, Sam grabbed his backpack off the floor and trudged up the steps of the lecture hall. He pushed open the door and burst out into the hallway, making Joe and Roxy almost run to catch up with him as he headed outside the building into the cool morning air.

Roxy began to cry. She wanted to sleep, but more than anything she wanted to understand her son. Seventeen years old, and most days she thought she was talking to a stranger.

"We were looking all over for you," she said, grabbing his arm. "We were so worried."

"Why were you looking for me?" he said, turning to face them. His eyes were sharp with frustration. "You know I've got work to do."

They got back to the truck and headed north towards the interstate. Joe pulled over at a Perkins, and they ordered breakfast. No one ate much. Roxy pushed her coffee back and forth on the table, every so often looking at her son as if she was about to say something, but then stopping short before the words came out. Sam picked at a short stack and watched the highway traffic whiz by below them. Joe used the pay phone in the foyer to call James and let him know. When he came back to the table, he stopped short; Sam had moved his chair closer to Roxy, the boy's head sunken into his mother's chest. They were whispering to one another, Roxy's fingers running over Sam's shaggy hair. Joe didn't move closer; he watched for a moment, then turned back to the lobby. He would wait awhile before going back. If they asked, he would say he'd been on the phone with James. He would sit down at the table and find his appetite again, forgetting exactly what he'd ordered. He would take whatever was put in front of him.

Song of Zekariah

Winter 2002

Trouble with most folks is they refuse to believe in miracles. Look around, brothers and sisters: we got about a hundred souls in this tent tonight, and if I asked each one of you your biggest problem, well, I'd probably get a hundred different answers. You got one problem: you don't believe in miracles. Oh, you believe there's a million dollars waiting for you in a bank in Nigeria, but you don't believe in miracles. You believe there's a pill to make you skinny overnight, but you don't believe in miracles. Brothers and sisters, you got to believe in miracles. If you believe in miracles, you believe in the Lord.

Anyone here wants to believe in miracles like I do, say Amen with me. Amen.

Blessed is the Lord, brothers and sisters. Blessed is the Lord God of Israel who raises the horn of salvation for all of us. If you hear the horn of salvation, you hear the Lord. Tonight that horn's going to shake the poles of this tent just like it shook the walls of Jericho. Tonight we're going to hear that trumpet blow.

Anybody wants to hear a heavenly trumpet so loud it shakes the fillings from your teeth, say Alleluia with me. Alleluia.

Tonight we're reading from the book of Jonah. Some years ago I was out in California preaching about Jonah, and after the meeting, a man comes up to me and says, "Brother Zeke, I like listening to you preach and tell stories and hoot 'n' holler and all, but I got a problem: I can't believe a fish could swallow a man and then spit him out three days later." I told him, "Then you *do* have a problem, brother, because that's not even much of a miracle. Far as miracles go, it's not even in the top ten. Heck, that don't even make my top hundred." Finding something to eat at my Nana's kitchen table back in North Dakota when you were late for Sunday supper, now *that* was a bigger miracle than a man getting spit out a whale.

Seems just about every town we visit across this great land has its own story of a miracle. Sister Betsy and I come from a little town in North Dakota you all never heard of called Nazareth. We got more coyotes than people, but even our tiny corner of the world has its tale. You see, one night there's a fight in the pool hall, and it spills right out into the middle of Main Street. Two young men in a gunfight over—what else, sisters?—a woman. I was only a boy at the time—can you imagine your Brother Zeke as a boy? Anyway, an old man of the town tries to get between these two hotheads and break it up. He's a good man, a pious man by the name of Ole Simonson. Well, both pistols go off, and old Ole gets it coming and going, *pow*, *pow*, two bullets right in the heart. People don't know who they should call first, the doc or the undertaker; the man must've been ninety years old. But you know what? The next day he's back on the farm, working the tractor like nothing happened. Why? A foolish man would say luck, but you and I know better. God wasn't through with him. God needed him, just like He needed Jonah. Just like He needs that boy at the train depot when he grows up to be a man. An old man of ninety dragged through Hell and then reborn—imagine that. I don't know exactly how many years Ole Simonson lived after that day, but I'd guess if you put the two oldest folks in this tent together and added up their years, you'd be close. You might be asking, *"What did God need an old man like Ole for?"* Well, that's between Ole and God. Just like Jonah's problem was between him and God. The Lord ain't much for gossip or hearsay, brothers: when He wants to tell you something, He tells you.

Anyone here ever bent their ear to gossip, say Alleluia. *Alleluia.* Now hold on a second while Brother Zeke says a couple extra Alleluias, because Lord knows I've told a story or two. Alleluia. Alleluia.

Why, just this morning I read about the baby hit by the train in some dusty Texas town yesterday. Talk about a miracle! You all probably heard about it, too: a mother standing on the train platform with her little boy in a plastic stroller. They're watching Daddy's train come into the station. She takes her hand off the stroller for a split second to fix her hair, and the unthinkable occurs: the stroller rolls onto the tracks, right in front of the oncoming train. The engineer stops as fast as he can, but the train drags that stroller for another two hundred feet or so. The mother is frozen in panic. Every single person on that platform thinks they've just seen a child die. They rush to the front of the train, and there they find the baby still strapped into his stroller, unharmed. Cranky as a newborn wolverine, but unharmed. The paramedics say all the kid needed was a nap. Now, if you don't see a miracle there, I think you do indeed have a problem.

Our friend Jonah had problems, too: He didn't end up in the belly of that whale by accident. He was a prophet who said no to God. Even an old prairie dog like me knows when you tell God no, you're going to have problems. Tonight, we're in the business of solving problems. Any preacher worth their weight in salty tears has to wear a lot of hats: he's in the listening business, he's in the shouting business. Sometimes he's even in the crystal-ball business. But more than all that, a preacher is in the problem-solving business. And tonight all I got to do is look at these long faces, and I know business is good.

Anyone here got problems stacked like pancakes, say Amen with me. Amen.

Now when Jonah comes out the whale, he's not looking too good. He's not smelling too good, either. Three days and nights inside a whale, imagine how you'd stink. Sisters, you know what they make perfume out of? That's right. Whale vomit. Now, the perfume makers give it a fancy name—*ambergris*—but you and I both know that's just putting lipstick on a pig, ain't it? These are the same kind of people who feel the need to call a plain old everyday toilet a water closet, or a restroom. Sisters, you know if you have kids, there ain't never no *rest* in that *room*. Back in my little hometown of Nazareth, North Dakota, a toilet gets called a toilet, a spade gets called a spade, and whale vomit gets called whale vomit. Yes, we call it like we see it in North Dakota. We know when you say *"l'eau de toilette"* you're saying "toilet water," and in our house the only family member uses the toilet water is the dog. But this ambergris is expensive stuff, sisters. Jonah's probably got fifty thousand dollars' worth of whale vomit on his clothes when he washes up on the white sands of Phoenicia. But he's a prophet, not a perfume maker. He knows he's got a job to do. When the fish sets him free Jonah says, "I will pay what I have vowed. Salvation is of the Lord." He realizes he had a problem of faith.

Anyone here besides me can't tell the difference between Chanel No. 5 and Aqua Velva No. 1, say Alleluia with me. Alleluia.

Most folks got the same problem as Jonah: you got just enough faith to make you miserable. You got the same relationship with God you got with the gas company, or the phone company. Once in a while you send them a check to pay your bill. God don't want your check, brother. When Jonah says, "I will pay what I vowed," you think he means cash or money order? Food stamps? No, brothers, no. Some of you probably go to bed counting your problems like black sheep in a conga line, and when you wake up in the morning you're still counting. You wake up with a face so long you could suck an onion through a straw. You forget to laugh. If I paid everyone here a dollar for every time you've laughed out loud the past week, I don't think I'd lose more than fifty cents. You know who can't laugh? That's right: the devil. He wants you to stay miserable. He don't want you to realize you only got one problem, and that's faith. He don't want you to know if you believe in miracles, suddenly you don't have any problems. If you get right with God, all those troubles that were stacked on your plate so high you thought you worked at IHOP—money and poverty, husbands and wives, sickness and envy—suddenly they don't weigh more than a hummingbird. That's faith, sisters: I've seen women take God into their hearts and walk out of this tent feeling like the Rose of Alabama, after twenty years of drink and debauchery made them feel like a Blackeyed Susan. That's faith, brothers: I've seen men walk in here like the Hunchback of Notre Dame, and when they take God into their hearts, they run back out like they play halfback for Notre Dame. Now, sometimes the Lord comes to you directly, like He did to Jonah, like Abraham and Moses and Elijah. And sometimes He speaks to us through the mouth of His holy prophets, who've been around since the world began.

Anyone here tonight wants to drop two hundred pounds of problems and float on out of this tent like a hummingbird, say Amen. Amen.

Ain't no pill going to do that, brothers and sisters. You can't buy faith. Ain't no layaway plan for miracles. Folks always ask me, "Brother Zeke, why do you go from town to town preaching the Word of the Lord, setting up your tent in parking lots and fallow fields when you could have your own church, your own congregation?" Oh, I've been to church, brothers. I've sat in those pews and looked at all those faces cold as stone. It felt like an indoor cemetery: the dead leading the dead. That's why we call this meeting a *revival*. It's a rebirth, just like Jonah is reborn inside the womb of that great fish. After three days, he rises again from his watery grave to go wherever the Lord tells him. Brothers, I'll preach God's word anywhere on this green earth. I'm like that book by Dr. Seuss: I'll preach on a boat, I'll preach on a train, on an airplane. I'll pitch this tent on top of a mountain and preach to the goats. I'll pitch it in the desert and testify to each grain of sand. And if they ever find a way to pitch a tent at the bottom of the ocean, Brother Zeke will be there too, testifying to all the wondrous beasts that crawl the ocean floor. Maybe I'll even be lucky enough to meet that old whale that swallowed Jonah, so I can tell him "how'do." But until then I'm going to keep on moving across this great land, listening to the amazing stories of faith and miracles you all have, and bringing the Word of the Lord to anyone who cares to hear.

Now Jonah's story don't end at that beach in distant Phoenicia. No, sisters, no. God tells him, "Arise, go to Nineveh, that great city, and preach the message I tell you." Basically, the Lord is telling him, get back to work. And boy, does Jonah have his work cut out with this one, because when you look up "den of iniquity" in the dictionary, I'm telling you there's a dusty Polaroid of old Nineveh stuck in there right beside it. Las Vegas is a convent compared to this town. Nineveh makes even the fabled Black Hole of Calcutta look like the pothole of Calcutta. Sodom and Gomorrah look more like Mayberry and

Mount Pilot. Trust your friend Zeke on this one: he's seen his share of dark corners of the world when he was in the Navy, and Nineveh was worse than all of them put together. And that's where God sends Jonah, to turn a whole city of sinners into saints, all by his lonesome. Now, you may be thinking, *good luck, Jonah.* You may be thinking, *God is setting this man up to fail.* I mean, here's this fella Jonah, seaweed on his head, smelling like whale vomit, skin bleached white from three days of soaking in the digestive juices of the great fish. When he shows up they probably won't let him inside the gates of the city, much less inside their hearts to repent and see the evil of their ways. But that's the ultimate wisdom of the Lord, brothers. Who shall He send to preach to a city full of idol worship, greed and vice? Fiery Elijah with a train of blazing chariots? Maybe Tom Cruise in a gold Cadillac? No, brothers, no. You don't put out a fire by sending in a tanker truck full of gasoline. The Lord sends the most humble preacher he's got, and that's Jonah, all right.

Now I can't go through a revival meeting on miracles without talking about my own miracle, or should I say, my son. How many moms and dads we got in here tonight? Praise the Lord. Yes, I have a son named Jan. He's studying to be a preacher, too, just like his pop, just like our old friend Jonah. These days you go off to college to become a preacher, imagine that? All those exams, pop quizzes, big old textbooks. When I was young, a man starting out on the kerosene belt only needed one book, brothers, the good book. But times change. Anyway, just the other day my son comes home from college and says to me, "Father, can I ask you a question?" Now, brothers, if you have sons, you're expecting him to say, "Can I borrow the car?" or maybe "When did you know Mama was the one?" but I guess the son of a preacher man sets his watch to a different clock, because what he does ask me is, "How will I know what God has in store for me?" Brothers and sisters, does that question sound familiar? I know it does. We ask ourselves the same thing, all the time: what does God have in store for me? My son has grown up to be a fine young man, humble and pious, ready to follow in his father's footsteps and preach the Word of the Lord. I tell him, "If God chooses you, you will be called the prophet of the Highest." If God chooses you, you will go before the face of the Lord to prepare his ways, to give knowledge of salvation to his people by the remission of their sins, through the tender mercy of our God, with which the dawn from on high has visited us, to give light to those who sit in darkness and the shadow of death, to guide our feet into the way of peace.

Anyone here ever ask God to help you do the impossible, say Alleluia. Alleluia, brothers!

Our friend Jonah tells the people of Nineveh, "You got forty days to repent." And you know what? They do, from the king right on down to the lowest stable hand. The story tells us, "The people of Nineveh believed God, proclaimed a fast, and put on sackcloth, from the greatest to the least." How did he do it? Nothing in my copy of scripture says anything about Jonah bringing balloons, a brass band, or a three-ring circus. Far as I know he doesn't give away a new car or a shopping spree with every repentance of sin. It's just him, a humble country preacher carrying the Word of God. It's just like I told my boy, Jan: if God chooses you like he chose Jonah, he's going to put you to work. Ain't no unemployment line when you're working for the Lord. But a preacher is only a messenger, brothers. A prophet can only get folks ready—ready for God to make good on the promise he made all those years ago. Even a prophet as mighty as Elijah or Isaiah don't have the power to save. They can only help blow that heavenly trumpet in hopes we'll be ready on the day the Lord decides to keep His ancient guarantee. I don't think I'm alone when I say I'm worried about the young folks these days, brothers and sisters. Maybe this is just an old preacher talking, but it sure seems like times have changed.

These days, oh Lord, how people hate to wait. You don't even have to get out of your car: drive-through restaurants, drive-through banks and liquor stores, heck, even drive-through churches. Remember how excited everyone was last year because it was a new millennium? People running around like chickens with their feet cut off because another thousand years had passed. Let me tell you, sisters, a thousand years is an eye-blink to God. A million years is a sip of tea. One second, God sees dinosaurs roaming the earth, and the next, He sees skyscrapers and satellites. Just this afternoon I was downtown in your fair city meeting folks, asking them to come to meeting tonight, and I met a young woman as she got out of her car. Before I could say a word she tells me, "Sorry, sir, don't have time." Now this woman has a car phone, she has a cell phone, she even has a phone just to call her other phones; she has so many gadgets I bet if you put some tin foil in her hair, she'd make a pretty good robot for Halloween. I ask her why she's in such a rush. She says to me, "I'm saving time." I tell her, "Just whose time are you saving?" Oh, she didn't like that. Not one bit. So as she walks away she tells me, "I've got better things to do than wait around for God." Waiting around for God! As if she was mad because the pizza she ordered didn't arrive in thirty minutes or less. Waiting around for God! As if God isn't already in every blade of grass and slab of concrete we walk upon, and in the very air we breathe. Waiting around for God! As if the Lord doesn't show us miracles every single day. A miracle is like a big billboard that reads, "Don't worry. God's coming." Sometimes we're too stubborn to look up and read the signs. If you want a sign, all you got to do is pick up your copy of scripture. Isaiah tells us in chapter seven, verse fourteen,

"Therefore the Lord himself will give you a sign: behold, the virgin shall conceive and bear a son and shall call his name Immanuel."

Let's check in on our old friend Jonah one last time. Now the city of Nineveh has been spared by the Lord; a hundred and twenty thousand souls given another chance at redemption. What does Jonah do next? He's done the impossible, he's completed his mission. It's Miller time. You might expect him to go right home and retire. Or maybe stay in Nineveh, and live the life of a local hero. No, brothers, no. What does Jonah do? He goes and sits on a hill outside the city and says to God, "O Lord, please take my life from me, for it is better for me to die than to live!" Can you believe it? On a lonely hill outside the walls of the great city, the prophet tells God he is ready to die. He sees the mercy bestowed on the sinners of Nineveh and knows he's no different; he's subject to the same judgment. God don't kill Jonah; the story leaves him sitting on that hill overlooking the city, hot sun beating down on his head. Now *this* is my kind of preacher, brothers. When the Messiah does come, I know he'll be a lot like Jonah: gentle and humble, not some glorious vision adorned in silver and gold. Now, an old buzzard like your Brother Zeke probably won't be around to see it, but I can still dream. You see, preachers don't die, they just run out of things to say.

When you walk out of here tonight, I want you to look for miracles. I want you to listen for those heavenly trumpets calling out for you. Can you hear them?

Say Alleluia with me, sisters. Brothers, say Amen.

The Death of John the Baptist

Summer 2010

The river always felt good on his bare feet. Jan walked out into the cool morning mud of the riverbank, feeling the smooth stones between his toes. The Little Missouri was more mud than water; by July farmers sat in the shade and told stale jokes like *folks got to drive to Minnesota just to remind themselves what water looks like.* By August even the alkali wells were only white sores crumbled on the landscape; anything that moved in open daylight was considered either crazy or on the run. Drought was an enemy older to the prairie than grasshoppers and doves, but the crops in North Dakota were a lot like the people who planted them: simple, but invincible to most anything, especially neglect.

The crowds at the river had been getting bigger. Only a year ago Jan would have found himself alone, once in a while coming across some kids swimming or a rancher watering his stock. But now they followed him. His father, the old tent preacher, would have been happy to see it. This oxbow had been the old man's favorite spot on the Little Missouri, a few miles downstream from the Allenby Bridge; old Zeke would practice his sermons under the big chokecherry tree while Jan splashed around in the water or rolled in the mud like a hound dog, escaping the summer heat.

It was days like this he missed his old man.

Jan shaded his eyes with his hand, squinting into the empty sky; another hour, and the sun would be high enough to find anything.

When he was a boy, summers in North Dakota seemed to last forever—until one morning, usually in early September, when everyone knew the world was about to change again. The morning air would suddenly turn cool, and thunderstorms would drift through the prairie, dumping new rain. But that was at least another month away.

"Already hot as Hades out here, ain't it?" a fat man called from the wilted grass of the riverbank. He was sweating through his thin white shirt and fanning his face with a straw hat. "You going to make it rain, preacher?"

"Wish I could," Jan said, looking up at the clear sky. "Right now, I guess the river's all the water we're going to get. You joining us?"

"Not today. You see, my name's Pastor Yarbrough."

Now Jan recognized him: Fred Yarbrough, pastor of the little country church over in Ambrose. He was with another man as thin as Yarbrough was fat, and standing together they looked like some sort of overheated comedy team. "I know who you are," Jan said. "Morning to you."

"This is Pastor White. His flock's over in Williams County." Yarbrough looked around at all the people getting ready, some already testing the river with their toes. "We've been hearing a lot about a preacher who calls himself 'Brother Jan' dunking folks out here at the river and, well sir, we wanted to see for ourselves."

"Welcome to you both," Jan said. "So, what do you see?"

"Frankly, this all sounds suspicious," Pastor White interrupted, his voice frigid. "People skipping services every week to come down to the river and get *saved*." He pronounced the word with thinly veiled sympathy, the same way one might pronounce *colon cancer*.

"Well, you know what Heraclitus said: *you can't step into the same river twice*."

"Is that right?" Yarbrough said with a thoughtful look, nudging the other man in the ribs. "You hear that, Carl? *Heraclitus* said that."

Pastor White wiped the sweat from his sallow forehead. "And I suppose now you're going to tell us the river is your church, or some baloney like that."

"The river's a special place," Jan said. He tried to smile, not wanting to let these two make him angry. At least he was amused at the fact he could remember anything from college, much less anything about Heraclitus. He could take comfort that his 3.9 GPA was finally paying dividends. *"My soul has grown deep like the rivers."*

Pastor White scratched his head impatiently. "And who said that? Socrates?"

From a little way down the bank, another voice rang out. "Langston Hughes."

It was Sam. He looked like he was on walkabout, his daypack and hiking boots both layered with red dust. His shorts and sleeveless shirt showed off the deep tan on his arms and legs. "Hey, cousin," Sam called over, taking off his sunglasses to rub the bridge of his nose. "Or should I say 'brother'?"

Yarbrough looked over. "Hey, I know you. You're the guy who built my roof. Davidson & Son, right?"

"That's right. The son, at your service," Sam said without looking at him, slipping the plastic bottle of water from the side of his pack and taking a drink. He stepped closer to the two pastors. "Why don't you go find some air conditioning somewhere? Looks like this man here's got work to do."

"We're men of God," Yarbrough said, puffing his chest. "We're the ones trying to do God's work."

"You're a brood of vipers," Jan said, dismissing them with a wave of his hand. "You don't realize it, but you need the river more than anybody."

The two men stood there for a long moment, not wanting to lose face. Slowly they both turned and made their way back up to the dirt road that led along this side of the river.

"I don't think they're too happy," Sam said, smiling. "Vipers?"

"It suits them," Jan said, folding his arms over his chest. "So, is this it? You finally decide?"

Sam smiled, shaking his head. "No, brother. I was just out here walking."

"You were just out here walking," Jan repeated. "Five miles from nowhere on the hottest day of the year, but you were just out walking."

Sam shrugged. "I like to walk."

"When are you going to decide?"

"Hey," Sam said sharply. "You know damn well I don't decide."

Jan nodded, looking down into the mud. "So you know Langston Hughes, huh?"

"Well, brother, I didn't go to college," Sam said. "But I do read." He rolled his pack higher on his back and started off, heading west towards a bald ridge.

Jan watched him go. He felt bad for showing impatience; he remembered what old Zeke used to say about waiting. But sometimes he couldn't help it; neither of them were getting any younger. They'd both turn thirty next year. He knew why people like Yarbrough had started to show up in person at the river; there were rumors going around that maybe this Brother Jan might be more than a preacher.

"Brother Jan," someone said softly from the riverbank. "I think everyone's ready."

At the top of the bald ridge, Sam stopped and looked down at the river; people had started to follow Jan out into the waist-deep water. From the hilltop he could hear the faint echo of their excited voices singing together. From a distance they looked like a string of bright pearls twisting across the brown water.

Lazlo Hooker got out of prison on a Sunday morning. It was already ninety-five degrees, but after two years inside the fence at James River, somehow the air felt a lot cooler on the other side. A breeze brushed the stubble on his shaved head as he stood by a lonely bus stop sign a couple hundred yards down from the main gate on State Hospital Road. In the distance he watched a big rig lumber east along I-94, the heat churning the air and making everything far away look like a mirage.

Speaking of mirages: he thought he saw his little sister in a subcompact idling in the visitor's parking lot across the road. He took a harder look, shading his eyes from the sun.

It was Daylene, all right.

The car crossed the empty road and pulled up next to him. She rolled down the window and gave him an icy stare.

Laz squinted in the sunlight. "I thought I was going to have to take a bus."

"If you don't get in before I change my mind, you still will."

She barely waited for him to climb in before she made a quick U-turn and headed back towards the interstate. "How's your habit?"

"I'm clean," he said right away. Lies always came quicker than the truth. "Mr. Clean, that's me. Even got the bald head to prove it." He rubbed the skin behind his ear. "Missing the earring, though. And the big muscles." He sat up straight in his seat like he was posing for a school picture. "How do I look?"

"You look like shit," she said, her eyes on the road. "But I'm glad to see you."

"How's Martha?"

"She's not going to talk to you," she said. "Mom neither."

"And where is the major these days? Antarctica? Katmandu?"

"Germany," Daylene said. "And it's the *colonel* now."

"Whoa, a promotion," he said. "She should be here, you know, picking up her son."

"You're lucky she still calls you her son. And you're lucky I still call you my brother."

"Hey, I don't have to take this abuse," he said.

"There's the door," she said. "Watch that first step, though."

Laz opened his mouth but nothing came out; he knew she was right. For a long time he sat silently, staring out his window as they drove the straight and shadeless arrow that was Interstate 94, a line unbroken by a turn or even a lane change. Endless rows of wheat and barley rolled past, interrupted every twenty miles or so by the lonely power lines that drooped off into the distance.

He'd like to tell her that part of his life was all over, that two stints in state prison had turned his life around, that he'd found his higher power, but she wouldn't believe any of it. He wouldn't believe it, either. Prison was a place where you had more secrets coming out than you did going in.

He rolled down the window and gulped the hot air blasting his face. They passed the green mileage sign that read:

BISMARCK	57
DICKINSON	112
WIBAUX, MT	258

He'd never even heard of Wibaux before, but it didn't matter. It was on the way to the West Coast, and that was enough. Pretty amazing, he thought: this road right here could take you all the way to the ocean in either direction.

"Let's just keep driving," he said, closing the window. He jumped in his seat with frantic energy like he was a kid again. "What do you say? California, here we come."

"Don't joke around," she said, rubbing the back of her neck. "My shift starts at noon."

"Waiting tables at the Flying J? Sounds like you're the one in prison."

"Look, I'm tired," she said. "Let's try to make it back to Bismarck first, okay?"

"What could possibly keep you here?"

"Don't push it, Laz," she said. "It's complicated."

"You still hang around that Sam guy?"

"What do you mean, *'that Sam guy'*? He's your friend, too. Or did you forget he put up your bail money last time?"

"All right, all right. Hey, you got a cell phone? I need to call some old friends."

"You don't got any old friends."

"Are you kidding? In this magical land of North Dakota, I'm like a king."

"If you use my phone to score drugs, I will kill you myself. Are we clear?"

"Le Roi est mort," he said wistfully, turning to stare out the window again. "Vive Le Roi." *Not the drugs you're thinking of,* he muttered under his breath. He was going to need drugs, all right, and these HAART cocktails were expensive; more than a truck-stop waitress and an ex-con could afford. He saw only one option ahead: dealing, which at thirty-two was his only job experience so far in life. He smiled weakly at the irony of selling drugs to buy drugs, a warped cycle of salvation. But the same weird logic in his head made him want to save his sister, too. Take her to California, Shangri-La, Atlantis, anyplace but here. "Look, I still know a bunch of people back there. All we need is the gas money."

"You want to go to California, you're going by yourself," she said. "I got about seven dollars in the bank you can have. But I'm staying here."

"All right, fuck California," he said. "You know what you need? France. That's it, the south of France: Nice, San Tropez, maybe a couple weeks in Marseilles." He clapped his hands together. "That's it—Marseilles. Big town with little streets, lots of sun. You'd love it."

She cracked a tired smile, too tired to keep arguing with her brother much longer now. She shook her head slowly, gazing down at her pale arms and hands attached to the steering wheel. "Yeah, I need to work on my tan." She was close to tears, rubbing her eyes with the back of a forearm. "For the last time, I'm sticking around, okay?" There was a long silence as she kept opening her mouth to say something, but it was hard to find a good starting place. It wasn't a story you could finish on a single car ride. She had a lot to tell him.

He folded his arms. "I don't get it. What the hell would keep you here?"

"Like I told you," she said. "It's complicated."

Sunday mornings at the Rooster, Elmer Scobey would leave a cardboard box for Jan on the counter packed up with leftovers: re-used plastic tubs filled with flannel hash and sausage links, half a flat of eggs, an extra gallon jug of milk about to expire. He had never been a church-going man, but he liked Brother Jan all right.

Elmer Scobey had been down to the river.

He sat on a stool back behind the grill nursing a cup of coffee and looking through the week's receipts. The old cat clock on the wall read noon; these days only one of its eyes moved back and forth, a creepy plastic cyclops. Sundays were only busy up until church time, so he'd let the girls go by eleven and look after any stragglers himself until he closed the Rooster at noon. He would've turned off the AC unit an hour ago to save money, but the sheriff's wife and her daughter were lingering at a back table. One thing he couldn't afford was bad blood with the sheriff. He'd go back out there in a minute to top off their coffees and drop off the check.

Out front, the bells on the door jangled as Jan came in and closed the door behind him. He was wearing that old camel-hair jacket that probably had more patches than fabric these days. He saw the box of food and looked around the near-empty café for its owner. "Thanks, Elmer," Jan called into the kitchen. "God bless."

"God bless you too, brother," Elmer called back from his little alcove. "Keys are in the ignition if you need my truck again to get out there." The preacher had been rounding up and delivering donated food to the migrant workers who came up for the summer harvest season.

At the back table, Sally Mae Rodriguez rescued herself from the boredom of sitting with her mother on Sunday morning by looking over the fuzzy young man at the counter. "Hey, that's Brother Jan, the preacher," she whispered to her mother. She'd heard all kinds of stories about Galilee County's very own hermit: that he lived in a cave, that he talked to animals just like Eddie Murphy in that movie. She knew he'd stood up against her stepfather about a dozen times. Sally tilted her head, taking him in; hermit or not, up close she decided he was kind of cute.

Her mother had been talking, but Sally had tuned her voice out long ago.

"Have you been listening to me?" Ingrid said, tapping her daughter's arm. "I was telling you a story about when I was your age and I worked here. Can you believe that? Me working at the Rooster."

"La-dee-da," Sally Mae droned, her eyes still on Brother Jan.

Ingrid Rodriguez looked up from her plate and followed her daughter's line of sight to the funny little man up front. "Some of the ladies in my bridge club can't stop talking about him. They say the river changed their life." She patted her daughter's arm again. "You know what, I'm going to invite him to supper. Lord knows we need some churchin' up in our house."

Sally Mae rolled her eyes. "Your husband says he's a troublemaker."

But Ingrid had already pushed her chair back from the table and stood up. "Brother Jan," she yelled, motioning with her thick arms like Jan was an airliner and she was pointing him toward the runway. "You must come over for Sunday supper tonight. I insist."

Jan smiled weakly and scratched at his scraggly beard. "Well, I—"

"No excuses now," she said, sitting down again. "We're having ham and my famous sweet potato casserole."

"Ma," Sally Mae said, rolling her eyes. "Brother Jan's a vegan."

"Is that a fact? A *vegan*," she said, pronouncing the word with slow wonder, as if it had been suddenly introduced from some faraway country like Lithuania or Mars.

"It means he only eats vegetables."

"I knew that," Ingrid said. "No problem, we'll just whip you up some mac and cheese is all."

Sally Mae giggled.

"Now what's so funny, young lady?"

"Macaroni and cheese ain't a vegetable."

"Macaroni and cheese *isn't* a vegetable," she said, reaching over and giving the side of her daughter's head a soft slap. "You mind your manners." She turned back to Jan, now a little short of breath. "You'll have to excuse my daughter. You'd never guess she just turned eighteen a couple days ago."

"Well, happy birthday," Jan said.

"Thank you, brother," Sally Mae said, leaning back in her chair and crossing her bare legs. "Did you get me a present?"

Ingrid got her breath back. "I've got it. How about a nice egg salad?"

Now the girl was laughing out loud; Ingrid stared at her daughter like she was a traitor on a sinking ship. "You hush."

Jan backed up a couple steps from the table. "Thanks for the offer, Mrs. Rodriguez. I do appreciate it. Got to get going, though. Busy day ahead." Before Ingrid could react, he had already picked up the box of food and was halfway to the door.

Elmer Scobey called to him from the kitchen. "God bless you, brother."

Ingrid watched the hermit hurry out the door. "Your daddy says he's a troublemaker. Says he's keeping a close eye on him."

"Yeah?" Sally Mae said, her eyes on the window. "Me, too."

"Anyway, I don't trust a man who only eats vegetables," Ingrid said. "It's not natural."

Sally Mae bit her lip. "He's kind of cute."

Ingrid put her fork down. "Why would you waste your time on a man who dresses like a juniper bush?" she said. "Smells like he sleeps in mud. Probably does. Anyway, he's taken."

Sally Mae turned to her mother. "He's got a girl?"

"You could say that," Ingrid said. "Her initials are *G-O-D*. Get it? You can't have him."

That's exactly why I want him, Sally Mae thought. She ran her hand through her long hair. "Just because he's a preacher don't mean he don't find me attractive as hell."

Ingrid sighed. "Young lady, you're playing with fire."

Sally Mae checked her cell phone for messages. "What else you want me to play with?"

"That's enough," Ingrid said, pointing to the door. "Now get out of here before I get mad and tell your daddy about the car."

"For the last time, he *ain't* my father," she said, not looking up from her phone. "He's my stepfather. And I could give a fuck." She started texting a friend, the corner of her mouth turned up in a wry smile. "You know how he looks at me."

"Don't be ridiculous. You think every man looks at you."

"They don't?"

Ingrid's face turned red as she fished in her purse for a few bills and threw them on the table. She pushed up from her chair and headed for the door, just as Elmer Scobey came out from the kitchen with a pot of coffee. They narrowly missed each other, Elmer side-stepping nimbly for an old man to avoid the head-on collision.

Sally Mae watched the choreography with amusement. Ingrid didn't stop, banging the front door behind her as she steamed out into the parking lot and the bright sun.

"Your mother's sure in a hurry," Elmer said. "Trouble?"

Not yet, Sally thought as she peered out the window. *Not yet.*

Fred Yarbrough stood in the pulpit of his church, pulling his damp shirt away from his skin. Every local pastor had shown up, even the ones long retired and gone to seed: men from Divide, Galilee, Williams, McKenzie. The oldest was Ben Runkle, who had been a chaplain in Korea and still had the hard jaw and sharp eyes of a man who had seen war. Usually these monthly meetings only drew a handful for idle chat over breakfast, but this was different. There were at least twenty men gathered in the pews now, all talking and arguing among themselves in animated voices like some sort of boondock parliament.

They had all heard stories about the river.

Yarbrough wiped his brow, sweating even though he'd turned up the air conditioning full blast a half hour before anyone else had showed up. "Brothers," he said, gripping the podium with both hands. "Just who is this Brother Jan?"

The room quieted. Most of the men looked around, waiting for someone else to start.

"There's been talk," one of the older men finally said, his voice filed down to a nub by age and cigarettes. "Some folks believe he's a prophet, the real deal."

"A lot of us knew his old man," another said. "Old Zeke was a fire-and-brimstone man, that's for sure."

Pastor White jumped up from his seat; he looked about forty, with short salt and pepper hair. He had a tiny one-room church in Grassy Butte. "Zeke was a tent preacher, all right. Smoke and mirrors. Obviously, the apple didn't fall far from the tree."

The room burst into a cacophony of voices again.

Yarbrough banged the pulpit with his fist. "Look, I got empty pews every Sunday. Half my congregation goes swimming down at the river instead of coming to church. Why don't they just lay out and get a tan while they're at it?"

Pastor White nodded in agreement. "I hear from the sheriff in Galilee he's already on the wrong side of the law, for Lord knows what. Probably inciting riots, disturbing the peace, who knows," he said.

"Where is Rodriguez?" an older man piped up. "I thought you said he'd be here."

"Should be," Yarbough said. "Point is, this Jan is a rabble-rouser, pure and simple."

"This is North Dakota," the man replied with a chuckle. "All we got is rabble."

Ben Runkle had been listening. "Excuse me," he said, rising slowly from his seat, leaning his arms on the pew in front of him. "If I'm not mistaken, Elijah was a rabble-rouser. Jonah, too." He licked his dry lips and drew a long breath. He carried the hangdog look of a man who'd spent a life telling people what they didn't want to hear. "But what if it's true? What if this Brother Jan is truly a prophet, sent by God?"

Pastor White laughed. "You can't be serious."

"Brothers, we all say we're men of God. We say our job is to prepare the way for the coming of the Messiah on earth. But what if the Messiah *did* come from a little town in North Dakota? Would we even know it?"

"Trust me, reverend," Yarbrough said. "Nothing good ever came out of Nazareth."

White folded his arms. "You think this man is a prophet? A true messenger of God?"

"You're missing my point," Runkle said in a slow and steady voice. "We all know it's been so long since the time of the prophets of scripture: Elijah, Jonah, Isaiah, Hosea, all those great shepherds of old. I'm not saying this Brother Jan is a prophet sent by God; I'm saying we wouldn't know what to do if he was."

A few of the older men nodded slowly in agreement, some mumbling to one another in low tones.

"I don't have to listen to this," Yarbrough said, stepping away from the pulpit. His face had turned red. "Go ahead and let your own church go out of business."

Runkle looked at him with a raised eyebrow. "What business are we in, brother?"

The room once again erupted in voices: some defending the old preacher's words, others mocking them. Yarbrough suddenly felt a chill run up his back from his damp shirt, as if from a draft of cold air.

Suddenly there was a loud voice bellowing from the back pews of the church.

The stranger had a thick, tangled beard and long hair; a pair of sunglasses held some of his greying locks back from his sunburnt forehead. He was eating an apple, enjoying it, chewing with his mouth wide open. Maybe he was lost; with his clothes, they took him for one of the motorcycle men they always saw on the highways in summertime, with his wrinkled brown chaps covering faded jeans and a denim vest thrown over a dirty t-shirt. His arms were thick and almost molasses brown from a lifetime of sun exposure. He looked comfortable, his boots propped up on the pew in front of him and his ragged head cocked back a bit as he chewed.

"You want to know if Brother Jan is more than a man," he said. "Am I right?"

Pastor White spoke out. "You know this Brother Jan?"

"Oh, I know him, all right. Known him since he was a baby. Seen him grow up. Seen him drive all your flocks down to the river, too." He took a last bite, licking his wet lips. "I want what you want, brothers: I want to know, is he just another impostor? Is he something more? Far as I can tell, there's only one way to find out." He tossed the apple core behind him onto the floor of the vestibule. "And that's to make him prove it."

"Excuse me for asking, stranger," Runkle said, still standing. "But do we know you?"

The man smiled, throwing his arms up in mock surrender. "Just a traveler passing through, reverend. Just a wayfaring stranger in need of some air conditioning; hot as hell out there, you know. Anyway, door was open." He stood up and slapped some of the dust off his battered leather chaps. "I didn't mean to break up the meeting, brothers. I said my peace." He sauntered down the center aisle back towards the door. "Just wanted the honest men of North Dakota to know you're not alone. One way or another we'll make him prove himself, don't you worry." He waved a gloved hand behind him as he kicked open the door with a boot, the sudden blast of sunlight making the other men squint and shield their eyes. "You all keep up the good work. Praise the Lord." Then the stranger disappeared outside in the bright light, the door clenching shut again.

A few moments later they could hear a motorcycle cough to life in the parking lot and slowly rumble away. A long minute passed before anyone opened their mouth. Yarbrough banged the pulpit again.

"Well, that seals it for me," he said. "If Brother Jan has friends like that, he's no man of God."

"Didn't seem like a friend to me," Runkle said, sitting back down on the pew, out of breath as if old age had suddenly caught up to him. "Seemed like an old enemy."

Anton Rodriguez sat in his cruiser with the motor running, his deputy, Bill Rolvaag, riding shotgun. Bill was along for the usual reason: the dirty work. Lately these little worker strikes could get ugly, thanks to that troublemaker Brother Jan stirring up all kinds of problems. Last week the preacher had two dozen of them walking in a circle in front of the county courthouse, holding signs and chanting songs. Now the hood of the car was pointed directly at Jan as he stood between the farm foreman and the twenty-odd *braceros* refusing to dig beets today. An old-timer named Joe Nathan owned the land, but Anton knew he'd never see him out here. The old men of Nazareth hadn't stopped calling his office, though, threatening his job if he didn't quiet things down. Which basically meant quieting down this upstart, Brother Jan. Anton had run other people out of town before—or rather, he'd gotten other people to do it.

"What are you thinking about, sheriff?"

"I was thinking about the last time I had the chance to run over a troublemaker with my car," he said. "Meth addict. Burned down his own damned trailer. Must've been ten years ago. Came at me like a crazy man."

"You hit him?"

"No," Anton said. "But a few days later he ended up just as dead."

Bill grunted. "Should've hit him."

They got out of the car, putting on their hats and pulling the brims down to shield their eyes from the naked sun. Anton pulled his trousers up around his belly as they got closer. Bill walked behind him, left hand already resting on his gun holster.

"About time," the foreman said. "Mister Nathan don't like this one bit."

"Why don't you just go on home, let these men work out their differences by themselves," he said to Jan. "You know, let the wheels of justice turn."

Jan folded his arms and squinted into the midday sun. "Wheels turn awfully slow in this county, sheriff."

"You don't say," Anton said, rubbing the stubble on his soft chin. "That Elmer Scobey's truck over there?"

Jan nodded. "He's good enough to let me borrow it from time to time."

"That so? Because it'd be a shame if we had to impound his vehicle. Part of the crime scene, you know. And this being Galilee County and all, where the wheels of justice turn awful slow, well it might be months before he got it back." He spat into the dirt. "Hopefully intact. But you never know."

As they talked, the *braceros* stood behind Jan in a loose circle and listened. There was an old man among them who had been staring at Anton ever since he had shown up. The old *bracero*, his gaunt face weathered from a lifetime of work, finally pointed at Anton and chuckled; his long, thin arms were like gnarled branches of some ancient tree. His younger companions turned to him with quizzical looks, wondering what could be so funny.

"You sound like your father," the old man said to Anton, his voice long ruined by cigarettes. "Yes, I remember *El Oso*."

Anton's face drew long. He looked away, his arms suddenly fidgety. "Well, thank you, I guess." Suddenly the warm air felt heavy, waterlogged with old ghosts again.

The old man stepped forward, his arm still raised. "You sound like him, but you do not look like him." He spat into the loose dirt. "Yes, you still look like *El Osito*."

A few of the other *braceros* heard the word and laughed among themselves. Anton's pockmarked face grew red, his cheeks still curved by the remnants of the baby fat he'd never really got rid of. He turned away and locked eyes with Jan.

"This is all your fault," Anton said to him. "Anything happens here, I'm holding you responsible. You hear me?" He spat in the dirt himself. "Let's go, Bill."

Bill pushed up his hat to scratch at his forehead, a look of surprise on his face. He stepped forward and grabbed the lapels of Jan's ratty coat with both hands. "Better watch yourself, brother." He gave Jan a shove and turned back toward the car, following in Anton's wake.

For Roxy, it had already been a day for ghosts. That morning, an invitation for James's wedding had come in the mail, and around lunchtime Lydia had sent a long and sentimental e-mail about Joe and her memories of growing up back in Cairo. And now at twilight she was returning to the house from a long walk, only to find Joe's ancient pickup parked half on the grass—just the way he used to leave it when he got home from work.

Sam waved hello from the porch.

As Roxy walked past the truck she ran her hand along the dents and grainy paint. She rested her thumb in a little crater near the front wheel where she could remember Lydia failing magnificently on her first driving lesson; Joe had taken her out in the middle of a fallow field, and she'd still managed to ram something, a cow feeder. Joe had come back laughing; he'd put a twin dent on the other side himself so the girl wouldn't feel so bad. It was moments like this, moments where memories would sneak up on her and make her heart stutter in surprise, that she missed Joe the most.

"I thought you sold this old thing years ago," she called up to the porch, trying hard not to cry. The smell of the cab took her back.

He nodded. "Thought it might have sentimental value."

"James is getting married," she said.

"Saw that," he said, holding up the invite in his hand, along with some other mail. He put it close to his face, trying to read the gold embossed lettering in the dim light. "Guess the fishing business is going good." He had a bottle of champagne next to him on a little table, along with a plate of half-eaten fried chicken. He sounded a little tipsy. "You think Cana, Wisconsin is as glamorous as Nazareth, North Dakota?"

"Doubt it," she said, making her way slowly to the top of the steps. "They got the Great Lakes, but we've got... well, we've got fried chicken and champagne." She was distracted, already staring at the manila folder Sam had resting in his lap, filled with all sorts of loose papers. Suddenly she had a feeling the wine and chicken were some kind of last meal. She leaned her shoulder against a post and wrung her hands tightly in nervous circles. "What you got in the folder there? Little early for taxes."

He put down the wedding invitation and lifted up the fat folder, handing it to her. "You probably want to keep all this someplace safe. It's got all the important papers: deeds, bank accounts, all that. I gave the business over to Eddie Gustavson. He's a good man. I told him to keep you in the loop, for old time's sake."

She didn't take the folder at first. "So, it's finally time."

He nodded. "I might not see you for a while."

"That's all you've got to say?" She grabbed the wine from the table and took a long swig straight from the bottle. She didn't know exactly what she wanted, but she knew she wanted more. "Son, I love you," she said, flopping into the chair beside him. "But you're really shitty at explaining things."

He didn't respond, just managed a feeble laugh.

The bubbles burned her throat. "I wish you hadn't told me anything. This would all be easier if I didn't know anything at all." She looked around the porch at all the junk that had accumulated there over the years: old bicycles, scraps of lumber, broken tools, Lydia's childhood dollhouse that had been long taken over by a local cabal of stray cats. Sam's crib, now filled with books. Sometimes she felt like the curator at a museum, living here alone, opening a random door or a cupboard to reveal some lost artifact from a completely different time, a different life. "God, I feel so lonely in this house. Sometimes I feel like the only woman on earth."

Her bare arms shivered in the cool evening air. Sam picked up his jacket and draped it around her shoulders. "Go easy on that stuff," he said, trying to pull the bottle from her hands.

She pulled it back and took another long swig, already feeling the slow boil of alcohol seeping into her blood. "Does Daylene know?"

He nodded. "I just came back from Bismarck."

"That girl's in love with you, you know." Her voice was more ragged now, louder with despair. "She'd better be, after ten years of this Mystery Theatre crap."

"She understands what I have to do."

Roxy gave him a sour laugh. "I doubt that. Take my word: a woman don't honestly understand much of anything if she's in love." She took another drink. "Do *you* even understand what you have to do?"

Sam sprang up from his chair, his voice stronger now. "Oh yeah, Ma, I got the instruction book right here. Picked it up at fucking Barnes & Noble. Then I went on fucking MapQuest and got the directions, too. Yeah, I'm good. I'm all set." He stood over her, his eyes hot with anger. After a while he let out a long breath, then ran both hands through his tangled hair. "I've got to go."

She stood up, reaching for his arm to pull him closer. "I'm sorry," she said.

"I'm sorry, too," he said, resisting her pull at first. His voice had dropped closer to a whisper now, his head hung low. "Sorry for a lot of things. You know that."

She nodded and they drew nearer to each other, Roxy wrapping her arms around her boy's shoulders. Sam stood with his arms at his side for a long moment, then slowly raised them to hug her back.

She had seen this exact scene in too many old black-and-white movies, where the mother catches the son on the front porch before he leaves for war; she wraps her arms around him, unable to let go. Then the boy breaks the embrace and the mother always says something stupid like, "Don't forget to write," instead of what she really wants to tell him. Even in *An Officer and a Gentleman,* a film she'd now watched at least ten thousand times, Debra Winger's mother lets her daughter leave the factory to start a new life with Richard Gere without telling her daughter much of anything. Roxy felt like that; all that was missing was the smart uniform.

She found herself unable to let go. Her son was leaving; almost thirty years coming, and still she wasn't prepared. Standing there on the porch, hugging him with all her strength, she realized she never would be. She realized she'd always been scared of being alone, terrified of spending time with only ghosts and shadows. She could remember the same fear sitting low in her stomach, all those years ago: driving away from a motel with a stolen child in tow, trying to get as far away from North Dakota as possible. Nothing had really changed since then: there would always be questions that had no answers. There would always be things left unsaid, promises impossible to keep. Joe was right when he'd told her she'd never get to really know her son, even though she'd never wanted to believe it. Now, she couldn't let go of him.

"Promise me you'll at least come to the wedding," she said, her tears making his shirt damp.

She could feel him slowly pulling away. "I don't know where I'm going to be."

"Promise me," she said, holding him tighter. There was something running in her veins that made her feel strong, something other than the alcohol. "Say 'I promise.'"

"All right," he said, finally slipping from her grasp. "I *promise*."

Roxy watched her son head toward the road, scrambling for something else to say. "Don't forget to write." She waved even though his back was turned. Without even thinking about it she mumbled the words "Go, butterfly, go" under her breath.

When he disappeared around the corner, she would go sit in the truck until she got sleepy. She would sit back in the passenger seat and dream, not because she liked it, but because it was all she had left.

Pressing her toes into the lukewarm muck of the river, Sally Mae couldn't help but think about all the slimy creatures that had recently crawled through the same ooze. That was one of the many problems she had with North Dakota: too much nature. She stood in the soft mud like a wading bird, her long, slender legs stretching in slow, measured steps toward deeper water. She doubted if the purple nail polish she'd bought at the outlet mall was sludge-resistant. Purple, the color of royalty; Sally's favorite, of course. And she felt naked without her cell phone, not wanting to risk getting it wet.

There were about fifty or so other folks gathered at the riverbank that morning, but they were all keeping their distance. They had their reasons: she wasn't wearing clothes. Not even a baptismal robe, just an oversized white t-shirt that draped above her knees. As far as they could tell, she wasn't wearing anything underneath. The gauzy shirt hugged her firm breasts and slender curves, billowing in the warm breeze. Everyone knew the sheriff's stepdaughter had a reputation for being a free spirit, but not this free, especially on Sunday. Most of the older women whispered to one another as the group slowly edged its way out to the middle of the river. Most of the men couldn't help but stare.

"What's the matter?" she called over to them. "Never seen a girl get saved before?"

Jan was already waist-deep out in the current with a couple of his closest followers; college kids mostly, spending their summer vacation following Brother Jan around the dry prairie and doing their best to live off the land. Sally couldn't understand why anyone would choose to do that, waste the summer on a big campout. Damn, they must smell horrible.

She had her own reasons for coming out here, of course.

"Sally," Jan said, surprised. "What are you doing here?"

"What does it look like?" she said. "Getting saved, of course." By now the river had splashed most of her t-shirt and made it translucent, leaving nothing to the imagination except a few inches below the neck. "I couldn't get my hands on a baptismal robe in time," she said, turning left then right in the slow current with her hands at her sides, as if modeling for him. She bit her lip. "I hope this is all right."

There was a long silence. Then, whispers started to filter among the crowd: *"Tramp." "Whore." "Spoiled brat." "Delilah."* All eyes were on Brother Jan, everyone jostling to get a good view of the prophet, everyone wanting to see firsthand what he would do.

Sally Mae was enjoying herself, for the moment at least. "Well, aren't you going to save me, Brother Jan?"

"Send that devil woman back to hell, Brother Jan."

With that, the crowd broke down into a mob of voices, some talking with one another and some simply talking to themselves in a cacophony of opinions, none saying anything remotely good about the sheriff's daughter.

"Don't she know she can't tempt a prophet?"

"She can if she's the devil."

"Listen," Jan said in a tired voice with his arms extended, trying to restore order. "I've told you before: I baptize you with water, but I'm no prophet. I'm no Messiah. I'm just a messenger. I'm only getting things ready for when the Messiah does come."

The crowd exchanged confused looks. *"When, preacher? When will the Messiah come?"*

"Soon," he said, distracted. Then Jan turned and glanced at each side of the river, as if expecting someone. "Soon, I promise. As for you," he said, turning back to Sally Mae. "Get on home. And grow up."

There were a few claps and muted cheers. *"Get on home, Delilah."*

Someone started singing: *"There's a hole in your bucket, Delilah, Delilah—there's a hole in your bucket, Delilah, get home."* Everyone broke out laughing, except for Jan, who kept his icy face.

Sally Mae wasn't used to anyone mocking her, at least not to her face. But she was determined to stand her ground, trying to put on a demure smile. "But—I just wanted to be saved."

Jan waded toward her until he was looking straight into her eyes, maybe half a foot separating them. "You don't want to be saved. You want to make a joke out of this. You want something to break your boredom. Well, you've had your fun. Now go on home. And for God's sake, put some damn clothes on."

She could hear some of them snickering behind her back. Then someone got the guts to splash her, then another. Soon a dozen people were pushing water on her, dousing her hair and face. She retreated toward the riverbank. "You're going to regret this," she said.

Even back on land, she could still hear them talking about her in low voices as she made it back to the riverbank. She cursed under her breath and jabbed her feet into her sandals and trudged up the embankment toward her car. As she reached the top, she felt someone watching her; she stopped, looking around to see a grizzled man in a cutoff vest sitting sidesaddle on his motorcycle. He was laughing to himself as he worked on rolling a cigarette in his gnarled hands.

"What are you laughing at?" she said, starting toward her car again.

"I got to say, he sure made you look foolish down there."

"Glad you enjoyed the show," she said, opening the back of her little hatchback and rummaging through a tangled mess of clothes. "How you could hear anything up here is beyond me."

"Oh, you'd be surprised how things carry out here. I always liked silent movies better, anyway—leaves more to the imagination."

"You sure talk funny," she said, slipping a wrinkled sweatshirt over her head. "Now do me a favor and fuck off."

"Honey, I'd be angry, too, someone treated me like that." He held the paper between his fingers as he cinched the sack with his teeth and stuffed it back into the pocket of his worn vest. "Question is, are you going to do anything about it?"

"What do you mean?"

"Well, your daddy's sheriff around these parts, ain't he?"

"Stepdaddy."

"Well then," he said, nodding his head. "I'm sure a talented girl like you can find a way. All depends on how bad you want it." He stood up and threw a leg over the bike, lifting it off the stand and turning the key.

"Who are you anyway, mister? You supposed to be in some kind of gang?"

He laughed, then ran his tongue along the edge of the paper. "Just a wayfaring stranger in this world of woe," he said, slipping the fat cigarette into the corner of his mouth. "And I'm pretty sure I know what you want."

The machine sputtered to life, and he rolled the throttle a few times, making a terrible roar that scared her at first. But she felt drawn to him in spite of the fear.

"Yeah?" She folded her arms. "And what exactly do you think I want?"

He lit the cigarette and nodded his head toward the bend in the river. "Revenge."

Bill Rolvaag had gone back to the truck to fetch the binoculars, but now he found himself completely lost. As the crow flies it must have been less than a half mile to the river, but the twisted arroyos made every direction look the same; drop your head for a moment and when you looked back up, the world was strange again. He tried to recall any scraps of orienteering they had taught him back in Cub Scouts—before he'd gotten kicked out for cheating on the pinewood derby, that is. He would be searching for moss on the north side of a tree, but there wasn't a tree within twenty miles, just scrub brush and endless folds of painted dirt on this side of the Little Missouri, the start of the Badlands. The high sun wasn't much help, either, since it was right around noon.

He cursed under his breath; losing an entire river was easier than he'd thought. But getting lost out here still beat a normal day on this job: sitting out on the highway, watching the cars go by. Or maybe getting lucky catching some kid with ten bucks' worth of meth tabs in his bookbag. He looked up into the darkening sky, half hoping for rain to break the heat. Ten more minutes of this, and he was firing off a round in the air.

The morning had been dry and clear, but now storm clouds were drifting in from Montana, draining the bright colors of the desert into a dull bone grey. As he peered up at the mottled sky he tripped and fell to the ground, his bare elbows breaking his fall. He looked down his leg at the suspected culprit: a tangle of old roots sticking out of the ground. *Fucking great*, he thought, lying there a long moment to catch his breath; he wasn't hurt, just dusty and mad at himself for being such a greenhorn out here.

He dusted himself off and scrambled up the side of a gully that looked familiar, binoculars slung heavy around his neck like a stone. They had been lodged under the driver's seat, and they looked like artifacts from some old war, the battered leather case engraved in gold with the initials *S. R.* He'd only had this deputy job for a few months but already he'd heard plenty of stories about Severo Rodriguez. None of them had said anything good. But hell, they'd named the local outlet mall after the guy, Bill thought; he must have been somebody.

He picked up his pace when he started to see the deep groove of the river valley grow wider in front of him; Sheriff Rodriguez's hat popped up about a hundred yards ahead, the fat man's hand waving at him. He'd probably chew him out for taking his sweet time.

Anton lay flat on his belly. "You get lost or something?"

Bill nodded sheepishly and took the field glasses out of the case. Putting them up to his eyes, he stood on the edge of the ridge and looked down. He got a fuzzy close-up of a clump of pigweed that must have been sixty yards off. He scanned up a bit until he found the brown shine of the slow-moving river, and then followed it until he could see the people wading below. The crowd had doubled since he'd ran back to the truck, probably at least fifty now, most dressed in flowing white robes. It was easy to pick out Brother Jan, since he was wearing the same ragged camel-hair coat he always had.

"Hey, your daughter's down there," he said, noticing the girl's long blonde hair as she waded into the water from the far bank.

"Stepdaughter, you mean. Yeah, I can see that much myself," Anton said, putting out his hand for the glasses.

Bill didn't budge, adjusting the knob for focus. A broad smile opened slowly across his face. "Oh yeah? Can you see she's wearing a white t-shirt?"

"So what if she's wearing a white t-shirt?"

"I mean, a *wet* white t-shirt. And far as I can tell, she ain't got nothing underneath." He grinned. "These binoculars *are* amazing, boss. I can zoom in right on her nipple." He adjusted the knob again. "Oh yeah, that's a nipple all right."

"Give me those damn things," Anton said, sitting up and snatching the binoculars from Bill's face.

Bill paced back and forth a few steps, excited now, taking off his hat to wipe the sweat from his brow with the back of his hand. "I got to get my ass to church more often," he said. "I mean, hot damn, they got a wet t-shirt contest going on down there."

"Would you shut up? And keep your head down."

Bill knelt on one knee. "Why are we sneaking around up here, anyway?"

Anton didn't have a ready answer for that, so he didn't say anything.

"There's a perfectly good road on the other side of the river, boss," Bill said. "We could be running tags while that Brother Jan and his sex cult splash around in the water."

"I told you to shut up," Anton said. "It's not a sex cult. It's a baptism. The preacher dunks them in the water to get rid of their sins."

Bill scratched the back of his neck. "Sounds like a sex cult to me. Like Charlie Manson."

"It's not," Anton said, rubbing the unkempt scruff on his chin. "But it could be dangerous." Last month he'd had twenty people down there. Now it was fifty. Next month it could be a hundred. Severo's ancient voice rattled in his head: *"You put a hundred folks together in Galilee County, you got an election."* Yes, he thought, this hermit preacher could be dangerous in a number of ways. He took one last look with the field glasses: Sally Mae was making her way back to the riverbank. The rest of the crowd was huddling around the preacher in a semi-circle. "Let's go. I've seen enough."

"Good timing," Bill said, looking up at the sky. "Just about to rain." He took the binoculars and gently put them back in the case, still admiring their power. He slung the case around his neck and took a last look down at the Little Missouri. "We going to arrest him, boss?"

Anton looked at his watch before starting off towards the truck. "I'm thinking on it."

Bill followed him, taking a can of snuff from his back pocket as he walked and pushing a wad of tobacco into his cheek. "Guess we need a reason, though, huh?"

"We don't need a reason, we just need an excuse," Anton said. "You work this county long enough, you'll know the difference."

The two men picked their way along the ridge.

"I heard you got to watch out for the rattlers," Bill said, looking down at his boots as he walked. He spit out a thin stream of chew. "You get out here often, sheriff? On foot, I mean."

Anton had to think about it. "No, not for a long time."

The entire sky lit up with lightning. A split second later, a massive clap of thunder rolled behind them; both men felt the shock ripple through their backs. Bill's stomach turned sour; he realized he'd accidentally swallowed the tobacco.

"Damn, that must've hit close," Anton said, stunned. Even his teeth ached from the thunderclap. "Must have been right over the river."

Slabs of rain began to fall, the sudden deluge quickly turning the top layer of dust into a slick sheen of mud in a matter of minutes, making their footing treacherous. Finding any landmarks now would be impossible.

"We must be close. You go that way," Anton yelled over to Bill, pointing down a long arroyo. "I'll try over there. First man to the truck, honk the horn."

The wind picked up, driving the rain sideways and stinging their faces. Bill's hat blew off into the growing darkness.

Anton stepped gingerly along the edge of the little canyon, his clothes completely drenched and glued to his skin. He got impatient and tried to move faster, but after only a few yards his foot caught on something and he fell hard to the muddy ground, loose rocks scraping the skin from his palms as he tried to break the fall. He let out a sharp yell as he hit, his knee throbbing with pain as it banged against something harder than dirt. Far as he could tell, though, nothing was broken. The rain began to die down as he rolled over on his back, making sure he hadn't lost anything from his pockets. Thick chunks of mud clung to his limbs. At least the storm had stopped just as quickly as it had started; darts of sunlight had already started to peek through the clouds.

When he sat up, he came face-to-face with a bleached skull sunk halfway into the ground. It was much too massive to belong to some stray cow or lost buffalo. The empty eye sockets glared at him with silent vexation.

Bill's voice called out. "Sheriff? You all right?"

Anton didn't answer. He tried getting to his feet, only to slip deeper in the mud. He searched for a foothold, anything for traction, but he stopped cold when his hand found something smooth and rounded sticking out of the earth. He looked down.

He had tripped over the half-buried end of a tusk.

"Sheriff, I heard you—hot damn, what is that?" Bill stepped closer, examining the long ribs that sprouted from the dirt like the frame of a forgotten house. "Sure is big. Looks like a dinosaur fossil to me, all right. What kind you think? Triceratops? Tyrannosaurus rex?" Bill had no idea himself, but those were the only dinosaur names he could remember from grade school. In high school he'd been to the state museum in

Bismarck when they had that new kind of dinosaur they found buried near Devils Lake, but he couldn't remember the name.

Anton kept silent, his hand gently rolling along the smooth contours of the skull.

Bill pulled his cell phone out of his pocket. "Hey, shouldn't we call the *National Geographic*? Maybe Animal Planet or the Pentagon or Steven Spielberg or something." He held it high in the air as he twisted his arm around in a circle. "No signal out here, go figure."

Anton picked up a rock and tossed it wildly at the sky, his ass still planted firmly in the mud. "Listen, it's not a dinosaur. It's an elephant," he said in a raspy voice. "These bones are only about twenty-five years old." He did the backwards math toward 1983 in his head. "Maybe twenty-six."

"How the hell do you know that?"

"Trust me," Anton said. "I know."

Bill stepped closer. "You sure you're okay?"

"Just go find the truck. Let me know when you find it."

Anton sat alone, his head churning with old memories. He had all but forgotten that night he'd seen the elephant. As a boy, there had been a stretch of months when he'd wake up in the middle of the night to study the map of North America taped to his bedroom wall with a flashlight. *How far did the elephant get today*, he would wonder. He'd trace an imaginary path with his finger, from the tiny black dot of Nazareth, North Dakota, to Seattle or Maine or Myrtle Beach or Tucson, Arizona. There was even a spot on the map called *Tuscaloosa*, Alabama—perfect for an African elephant in need of a few small repairs. He'd picture the elephant traveling by moonlight, crossing highways, mountain ranges, swamps, deserts, golf courses, parking lots, lonely fields of corn and cotton and winter wheat. He would imagine it ducking into alleys or slipping behind billboards to avoid being spotted. He would scour the newspaper and the evening news for any word of an elephant popping up, but there was never any word. He'd always just believed the elephant had made it.

Truth was, it hadn't made it very far at all.

Elmer Scobey knew he was late getting to the river. When he spotted the Allenby Bridge up ahead he gunned the engine, barely slowing down to make the sharp turn onto the dirt track that shadowed the riverbank. He didn't expect to see the motorcycle coming the other way; in a split-second Elmer pulled hard on the wheel and slammed the old brakes, almost taking the truck into the water and missing the bike by inches. The motorcycle didn't stop or even try to swerve; Elmer watched in his rearview mirror as it just swooped onto the highway like a lazy bird and headed toward town, the rider's hippie hair and vest fluttering in the breeze.

Elmer managed a smile; now even Hells Angels were coming down to the river. That Brother Jan must truly be a miracle.

It was already looking to be a strange day: the morning had been cool, signaling the end of a long, hot summer, and now there were stacks of fearsome clouds moving in from the west. At least the farmers could use the rain.

Both of the girls who worked the Rooster had called in sick, so he had to work Sunday alone, including washing all the dishes left in the sink by closing time.

"*Strange days indeed,*" he sung to himself as he put the truck in reverse and backed gingerly onto the road. "*Most peculiar, Mama.*"

The weather was moving in fast as Elmer reached the bend in the river; he noticed there were more cars this time. He pulled the truck into the dry sawgrass along the road and jumped out, expecting everyone to already be out in the water.

But as he side-stepped down the embankment he saw everyone standing silent on the riverbank, looking out on the water. Everyone's clothes seemed dry; no one had been saved today.

"What's going on, friend?" Elmer asked a man he'd seen down here before. The man looked at him with a blank stare.

There were two men out on the river. One was Jan; Elmer identified him easily from his clothes and crazy hair. The other man he didn't recognize right away. They were talking to one another.

He watched as Brother Jan put his palm on Sam's head and pushed until his body disappeared into the still water.

Lightning struck directly above them, the entire sky suddenly bleached white. A clap of thunder shook the ground. On the far bank, the thunder had shook an arc of wild doves out of the tall grass, scattering the birds like snowflakes on the wind. Rain started to fall in sheets, sending most of the crowd searching for cover. Elmer didn't move, his eyes fixed on the river.

Elmer watched Sam wade to the opposite bank and disappear into the desert. The people in the crowd came back to the river as the rain tapered off, not sure what they had just witnessed. Jan came back to them, drenched to the bone but smiling.

"Isaiah said, '*Make straight the way of the Lord*,'" Jan said, mostly to himself. He was still ankle deep in the river. He took a deep breath, looking around the riverbank before he lifted himself out of the water as if he were about to set foot on an undiscovered land. "And so it starts."

The crowd had already broken out in confused chatter. "*What* starts, preacher?" a woman called out to him.

"You don't follow me anymore," he said, a sense of relief in his voice. "You follow *him*."

Elmer helped the preacher out of the water. "But ain't he going the wrong way? All there is out there is desert."

Jan put his hand on the old man's shoulder. "It's the *only* way," he said, smiling.

For the first time in his life, Anton Rodriguez was drunk. In forty-two years he'd felt tipsy on occasion, maybe even a little light-headed, but never completely plastered like this; the memory of Severo Rodriguez had been enough to scare him away from the bottle. But now it seemed his father's life seeped into his own a little more each day, like water finding the cracks in a dam. He could still feel the old man's whiskey breath beating down on his face, the stench of hot sulfur and sour milk. More than anything, it had smelled like loneliness.

This is how Severo had spent the last half of his life, inside a bottle.

Andy's Place was empty; it was a hot Sunday afternoon, and Anton had parked the sheriff's cruiser right in front, and that probably had a lot to do with it. Even the bartender had stepped out for what must have been an extended smoke; Anton hadn't seen him for at least a half hour. It was dark inside with the shades drawn on the front windows, the only real light coming from the beer signs behind the bar. The video jukebox that hung on the back wall whipped out annoying patterns of whirling red and green light, making the old parquet ceiling look like some kind of weird Disco Borealis.

Technically Andy's didn't open for another hour, but this was never a place for regular hours. The chairs were still stacked on the tables. The lone AC unit above the front door chugged patiently. Anton sat at the bar, tipping his stool forward every so often to grab the well bourbon and top off his glass. It tasted terrible, but he was beyond tasting now. If the alcohol didn't put him out, the Xanax eventually would.

What he wouldn't give to be a kid chasing elephants again.

Growing up, he'd always told himself the last thing on earth he would become was Severo Rodriguez. And yet, here he was, a middle-aged replica of his father: the pot-bellied backwater sheriff with no friends and only a hollow shell for a family. Now he even had acquired the old man's breath. How did a man end up in the exact spot he wanted to avoid? Maybe life was simply a funnel after all, he thought: a long killing chute that herded everyone single file towards the abattoir. He could recall a lifetime ago when Mr. Deegan had told him *life is about choices*, but choice was bullshit if there's only one exit. Maybe the only difference was what happened in your dreams, he thought, when you were asleep. Dreams and nightmares.

Anton raised the glass to his lips again and swallowed hard. *"Here's to choices,"* he mumbled. *Here's to Mr. Deegan.*

His eyes closed.

He is sitting in the back of Mr. Deegan's class, admiring the shiny hair and slender shoulders of the girls in front of him. He has a crush on Ingrid, his brother's girl, but just about everyone else in Nazareth with a pulse does too. Anton sits in his Formica desk and pretends to listen to a speech on the Battle of Waterloo, but he's really dreaming about marrying Felipe's girlfriend. He has no idea what marriage is. At sixteen it sounds like heaven. He tries to sit with Ingrid in the lunch room, but the older girls laugh and shoo him away like a stray dog. Her feathered blonde hair is like spun silk. Her legs are crossed underneath a plaid polyester skirt, but as soon as school ends she's in the parking lot, smacking Hubba Bubba and wearing Jordache jeans. She's got a faded t-shirt with no sleeves and the black boots someone told her makes her look just like Lita Ford. She's waiting for Felipe to pull up in his dirty truck so she can throw her bookbag in the back and ride shotgun around Nazareth like a queen hanging onto a parade float, dancing in Felipe's bucket seats to the radio, bobbing her slender neck to the beat.

His eyes opened, but part of him was still wrapped in the warm fog of a dream.

Behind him, he barely noticed the front door to the bar squeaking open. He figured it was the bartender, coming back in to finish opening the place, but instead there was the surprise of sharp heels clicking on the tired linoleum. Then, a girl's voice: "So, what are we drinking to?"

He wobbled the stool around in a crazy orbit, trying to keep his balance. It was hard to focus in the dim light, with or without the booze and anti-depressants oozing through his blood. He was still in his dream: eighteen-year-old Ingrid stood right there in front of him, hands on her lithe waist, ruby lips smacking a wad of bubble gum. Somehow Ingrid was a girl again, and she was looking Anton over with a curious eye.

"Never seen you like this before," she called out, moving past him to the bar.

"Ingrid," he said in a raspy voice, his throat suddenly dry. He reached out his arm.

"Close," Sally Mae said, tossing her keys and phone onto the bar. "You really *are* wasted, aren't you?" She crossed the floor over to the jukebox.

His eyes trailed her as she walked, mouth open but nothing coming out; he was still unsure how to talk to ghosts.

The girl pushed the buttons on the machine, flipping through songs. "Hot damn," she said. "They really need to update this thing if they ever want anyone under eighty buying a drink in here." She kept pressing the buttons and tapping her nails against the glass. "I mean, what the fuck is a 'Blue Oyster Cult'?"

Anton turned back to the bar, the rush of hallucination wearing thin for a moment. "You're not allowed in here," he grumbled, still too drunk to notice this was the first time the girl had never called him by his first name. He sputtered impatiently over his shoulder. "What are you doing over there?"

"Trying to find something to dance to, of course," she said, still leaning on the jukebox, the round edge of her ass sticking out from under her little skirt. "You *do* want to see me dance, don't you?"

"I want you to go home," he said. He downed the rest of his glass, then poured some more liquor. He missed the glass with the bottle, whiskey puddling on the polished wood of the bar. Suddenly the room began spinning like a tilt-a-whirl. He dropped the bottle and it rolled down the bar, spilling everywhere. He grabbed at the edge of the bar with both hands to stay upright, but he felt the pull of some dark undertow. The tilt-a-whirl was going faster, the rest of the carnival around him becoming nothing more than a blur, the faces of people waiting in line below bleeding into one another like chalk drawings left out in the rain.

He could taste the cotton candy. He could hear the fortune-teller.

He put out his hand. "Do you want to go see the elephant with me?"

Sally Mae looked at him, giggling. "I don't know about any elephant," she said, running a hand through her long hair. "But a little bird told me you saw me at the river the other day."

"A little bird," he mumbled, eyes almost closed. Then his head jerked up, as if pulled by a string. "Wait—what were you doing at the river? Was Felipe with you?"

Sally had already turned back to the machine, pressing more buttons. "Here we go," she said, letting out a little whoop. "My faith in this dump is restored since they got some old Liz Phair on this thing—even if it is buried under all this honky-tonk crap." She smiled. "I love this song. You got a dollar, Anton?"

He looked at her with half-moon eyes, his head sagged to one side.

She moved back across the floor toward him, taking her time. "You want to watch me dance?"

His red eyes opened wide and studied her face. The room was finally becoming clearer. "But you're my—"

She shook her head. "I'm whatever you want me to be."

He looked nervously to the door.

Sally came closer, draping her arms on his shoulders. "Don't worry," she whispered into his ear. "I locked it when I came in." She reached past him and plucked one of the loose bills he had scattered on the bar. As she stood back up her breath brushed his neck, making him quiver. "I'll take care of you tonight, don't worry," she said, touching his cheek. "Our secret."

Sally Mae went to the jukebox and fed in the dollar. In a moment the place was filled with the lazy rhythm of a blues song. She slid back out onto an empty spot on the floor, sliding her hips to the slow beat, her fingers moving up her body, tugging on her shirt, wrapping around her neck. "So," she said, her voice much softer now. "You want to see me dance, don't you?"

He didn't care if Felipe found them now. She looked so beautiful. He didn't care about anything. "Yes," he said, his throat so tight he could barely get the word out. "Yes."

"*Good*," Sally Mae purred, a Cheshire smile across her face now. "If I dance for you," she said, turning around slowly, her thumbs edging down the waist of her skirt enough to show off the rose tattoo at the small of her back, "what do I get?"

Anton watched the lights from the jukebox pass over her body like veils. The undertow had him now. "Anything you want," he said, gasping for air as if drowning.

"Anything?"

He lifted his hand and reached for her. She danced closer.

"Yes," he said, almost choking now. "Yes. Yes. Yes."

Bill Rolvaag looked into the rearview mirror as he turned the car around on the narrow dirt track, keeping an eye on his new prisoner slumped in the backseat. The sheriff had called him at home an hour ago and told him to arrest Brother Jan. Rodriguez hadn't given a reason, and he hadn't stayed on the line long enough for an answer. He definitely sounded weird. Bill was pretty sure it had something to do with what had happened the night before: he'd been sitting in Andy's Place drinking a beer and playing the keno machine when Sally Mae came in and started talking to him straight away, which made him nervous because she'd never paid him any attention before, and here she was hanging on his shoulder at the bar like she wanted his autograph or something. After a few drinks and some heavy petting she asked if he'd do her a little favor. She whispered it into his ear, "I want you to do something to scare that asshole preacher Brother Jan."

"Like what?"

The girl slipped onto a stool and sat there for a moment; he could hear the gears in her head working. "I don't know, put him up against a wall or something. Make like you're going to run him over with your car. Shit, arrest him if you have to."

"Gladly," he told her. "I'd need a reason, though."

She leaned into him. "I could give you a reason."

"I'd need a better reason than that," he said, giving her a broad smile. "Like, one that would let me keep my job." He'd heard all about what had happened at the river between her and the preacher; hell, everybody within fifty miles had heard about that. And she was cute and all, but he didn't have to do much math to realize she wasn't worth losing the one thing he liked doing more than anything: being a lawman.

As expected, she didn't stay much longer. Obviously, Bill thought, she must've persuaded her old man on it, because here he was at twilight on a Sunday putting the smelly son of a bitch in the back of his cruiser and taking him to county jail. It hadn't taken long to find him; everyone in Galilee County knew you'd find him down at the river on Sunday.

At the moment he didn't feel much like a lawman, more like an errand boy sent to fetch the luggage. He felt like a minor character in a book or a movie, the guy who you see just long enough to bring in the soup or answer the telephone before the real characters, the real people, come on. Looking in the mirror again, he felt kind of sorry for the hermit now.

"Well, looks like we got a full jail tonight," he said, trying to break the silence. "We got you, and then we got this drifter I picked up this morning."

Jan looked out the dirty window at the river. "Didn't know drifting was a crime."

Bill laughed a phony laugh. "You got a sense of humor, that's for sure. No, I got him on reckless driving. Guy was trying to be Evel Knievel, right there on Main Street. Damn bikers think they own the road. Almost begged me to lock him up." Bill had been sitting in his car drinking coffee that morning when the bike had ripped past him doing at least a hundred, then turned around down by the courthouse and came back for another run. "Almost forgot, he was asking about you. Says he knows you. You don't know any bikers, do you preacher?"

"You still haven't told me why you're arresting me."

Bill shrugged. "Boss tells me to do something, and I do it." He picked up his cigarettes from the front seat and held them out, but Jan waved them off. "Yeah, well," Bill said. "Least you'll have someone to talk to. Should be real cozy, with the one cell." Bill turned his head around and attempted a smile. "Who knows, maybe you'll make a new friend."

Suddenly Jan jumped in his seat as if something had bit him, leaning forward to put both hands on the metal grille. He'd been put in the jail before, but this felt different. "This biker. What does he look like?"

"I don't know, your typical biker type I guess," Bill said, trying to remember. "Big guy, probably mid-forties. White hair in a ponytail. Talks a hell of a lot, I'll tell you that." He slowed down as they reached the highway. "So you do know him?"

"Yeah," Jan said with a sigh, settling back into the seat. "I might have seen him around." Then he kept silent, turning to look at the river as it disappeared behind them.

Bill watched him in the rearview as the cruiser picked up speed on the empty highway and headed towards Nazareth. "Don't worry, preacher, you'll be back at the river again in no time."

"I don't think so." Jan turned back around, closing his eyes as if ready to sleep. "I got a feeling I'm never going to see the river again."

The Temptation on the Mount

He ain't making it out of that desert alive.

I do my best work in the wasteland. Ain't no accident old Moses never made it out of the desert alive, all those years ago. Old fool never got to set foot on his precious promised land. Every soul's a martyr in the desert. I seen entire cities swallowed by sand, whole armies disappear into dust. These Badlands hold their share of bleached bones, and tonight I'm going to make sure there's one more carcass left for the buzzards and worms.

I've made mistakes before with the lives of men. Was a time when I was sure Abel would slay dimwitted Cain; I can remember putting my money on Esau and not his sly little rat of a brother, Jacob. I still cringe when I think of placing my bet on Goliath wiping the floor with David so the boy-king would become a martyr. Thought Joan of Arc would live to be an ugly old maid, not burned alive as a teenager. And I was damn sure the Nazis would be first to build a bomb and erase New York and London. But the lives of men ain't worth much. After all, what's scripture but a long and stale list of the dead.

Tonight I'll make certain this Sam Davidson is the One. It's going to take more than magic bread or a burning bush to keep him alive.

Tonight, the Messiah's going to die. Long live the Messiah.

I ain't without pity; I admit I had the wrong guy all along. And I admit hanging yourself in a jail cell is a horrible way for a man to die. With any luck the bumbling sheriff will take the blame; maybe the deputy, maybe the spoiled little stepdaughter. I guess it don't make a difference in the end; sooner or later folks tend to fill in the blank spots of a story anyway. Sometimes a story's defined by what's left out. Any tale depends on the empty spaces in between.

Tonight I'm going into the Badlands to test his pride. I'll say to him, if you are truly the Son of God, prove it. Turn one of these dusty desert stones into bread. Jump into the deepest arroyo and let the angels break your fall. Show me you're the Chosen One. Show me you're prepared to die for this world, and not just another loudmouthed mortal whose death comes too easy.

Tonight when he's broken down with dark loneliness, I'll take him to the top of the tallest skyscraper and tell him to look down. I'll say to him, all this could be yours. You really want to die so young? You really want to leave this earth without seeing the Yukon or the Himalayas, without knowing what it feels like to dip your toes into the mighty Amazon? You really want to say good-bye to that pretty girl you love with all your heart?

I'll tell him, all you got to do is kneel before me and I promise you'll live forever. All you got to do is open your eyes and let me show you the possibilities. All you got to do is listen.

Listen, and you'll hear the story of one world just beginning, while another comes to an end.

Tommy Zurhellen was born in New York City. With the help of the GI Bill, he earned an MFA in fiction writing at the University of Alabama. His stories have appeared widely in journals such as *Carolina Quarterly, Passages North, Quarterly West and Appalachee Review,* and his work has been nominated for the Pushcart Prize in fiction. He teaches writing at Marist College in Poughkeepsie, New York.

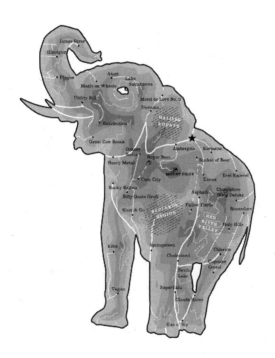

A NOTE ABOUT ELEPHANTS

The elephant has long been a powerful symbol of wisdom and strength, particularly in Eastern religions such as Hinduism, where the god of wisdom, Lord Ganesha, is depicted as having the head of an elephant. Since ancient times the elephant has been a symbol for the birth of the Buddha, and in Thailand and Burma, the white elephant is still considered holy. Elephants were trained for warfare as early as 2500 BCE and used most famously by the Carthaginian general Hannibal, who conquered Rome with an earth-shaking armada of armored war elephants.

In rural America during the 1800s, the phrase "seeing the elephant" became a metaphor for being left speechless, due to the rare experience of actually seeing such an exotic and magnificent creature up close when the circus came to town. It also came to mean a humbling loss of innocence; "I've seen the elephant" was an admission of some sort of epiphany or change of heart. And in the early 20th Century, Jack London introduced the term "pink elephants" to the American lexicon, which has since come to mean hallucinations brought on by alcohol abuse.

In *Nazareth, North Dakota*, Anton Rodriguez' loss of innocence begins when he witnesses the elephant's escape from the carnival; Severo and Felipe see it as merely a nuisance, but to Anton, an elephant set loose in North Dakota becomes a symbol of wonder and independence. Years later, when by chance he stumbles upon the elephant again, he finally realizes all he has lost by following in the footsteps of his father. And when Ole Simonson comes across the escaped elephant at the river, even the oldest man in the world is surprised by something he cannot describe in language. Roxy's lifelong struggle with alcohol, in essence, makes her "see" her own elephant and provides the story with yet another connection to this ancient and mighty creature.

SPOILER ALERT

(To Be Read Upon Completion of *Nazareth, North Dakota*)

List of Characters

Many of the characters found in *Nazareth, North Dakota* are inspired by people found in the New Testament accounts of the young Messiah. Below are brief descriptions of select characters; the biblical personality upon whom the character was loosely based is in parentheses.

Roxy Boone (Mary) is a hot mess. She's a 31-year old alcoholic in a bad marriage, but she has a good heart, and she desperately yearns for some kind of redemption. She gets a chance when someone leaves a baby on her doorstep at a seedy North Dakota motel called Motel de Love No. 3.

Sam Davidson (Jesus) is that baby, and he just might be the Messiah. From the start, it's clear he's no ordinary kid, and we're not just talking about superpowers. As with the Bible, we see him growing up through others' eyes, leaving a lot to the readers' imagination. He's a mystery at this stage of his young life, but he's biding his time until his time comes.

Joe Davidson (Joseph) is the big-hearted carpenter and father of two who falls in love with Roxy and Sam, too. He becomes Sam's step father, but for such a big man he's unsure of how he fits in, and how to talk to such a boy.

Severo Rodriguez (Herod the Great) is the grizzled old sheriff of Galilee County, a bitter man who is after Roxy and her mysterious new child. He rules the county with an iron fist, and is convinced one of his sons will take his place as the unofficial "king" of this lonely corner of the world.

Anton Rodriguez (Herod Antipas) is Severo's youngest son, a pudgy boy who grows up to be sheriff of Galilee County after his father's death. For better or worse, he's nothing like his father. He has a lifelong love for his older brother's girl, Ingrid, and his memories of childhood haunt him forever.

Daylene Hooker (Mary Magdalene) is new to Nazareth, North Dakota, where her family transplants as she is beginning her junior year of high school. She is small but scrappy, and not about to take any of the guff from the local girls who see her as some kind of oddity. She meets Sam and his cousin, Jan, and finds herself falling for one of them. Later, when Sam moves away from Nazareth to start teaching along the shores of Lake Superior, Daylene will find herself still drawn to him, even if it means dragging her loafing brother along with her.

Lazaro Hooker (Lazarus) is Daylene's older brother and defines the term "fish out of water" when he finds himself living in a small North Dakota town. Years later, he will die a young man but no miracle is out of the young Messiah's reach, including the raising of the dead.

Jan Olafson (John the Baptist) is the son of a preacher man, and 100% nerd. But he's also the closest thing to a friend that Sam has got, and he's going to be a big part of what's to come. He doesn't know it just yet, but there are some elements in town that would prefer he was dead, including the local pastors and the precocious stepdaughter of the local sheriff,

Sally Mae Rodriguez (Salome) is Ingrid's daughter and rebellious stepdaughter of the sheriff, Anton Rodriguez. She sets her sights on the local hermit, but when she is humiliated and spurned, all she has left is vengeance. She's a beautiful eighteen-year old girl; she knows how to get her revenge.

The story of *Nazareth, North Dakota* ends with Sam going out into the desert alone to be tested by the Devil, but of course the story of a young Messiah doesn't end there. Introducing some of the new characters forthcoming in *Apostle Islands*, the sequel to *Nazareth, North Dakota* (due Summer 2012):

Simon "Rocky" Romack (Peter) is a fourth-generation fisherman who runs the family fishing operation along with his little brother, Andy. He owns four boats and a lifetime of problems. His marriage to June is on the rocks and his mother-in-law is dying of cancer. But when a young guy named Sam Davidson shows up one summer on the shores of Lake Superior, he knows his life will change forever.

Judd Sackett (Judas) is a member of one of the many militia groups that call the rural landscape of the upper Midwest home. His talents lie in organizing and fund-raising, and when he meets Sam Davidson he knows exactly how to get people to listen, even if he doesn't necessarily agree with the message. Is he the one to sabotage Sam's mission, or was he made the scapegoat by someone else who thought they'd gone too far?

Jimmy and Johnny Thunder (James and John, sons of Zebedee) work the dock for Romack Fish by day, but their real passion is professional wrestling, jumping off turnbuckles just about anywhere there's a ring. They're good boys with wild streaks far too long and wide for a small town. Are they ready for a real shot at redemption instead of the cartoon version?

June Romack (Junia) has been married to Rocky since high school. She's tired of a life that always smells like fish, but never thought about another life, until now. The circle forming around this Sam Davidson seems to be exclusively a boy's club; what they need more than anything is a female perspective.

Keifer Conway (Caiaphas) is the local circuit judge desperately seeking reelection. When a case of one Sam Davidson ends up in his courtroom, charged with a plethora of crimes that all reek of un-American values, will he use it as a way to gain votes or will he have to hand the case over to an even higher authority?